SHADOWS

A Bayou Magic Novel

KRISTEN PROBY

Ampersand Publishing, Inc.

Shadows
A Bayou Magic Novel
By
Kristen Proby

SHADOWS

A Bayou Magic Novel

Kristen Proby

Cover Design: By Hang Le

Published by Ampersand Publishing, Inc.

Paperback ISBN 978-1-63350-049-5

A NOTE FROM THE AUTHOR

Dear Reader,

If you've read me for any length of time, you know that I love a love story. Telling love stories is what I'm most passionate about. Over the past couple of years, I've wanted to dabble in a little suspense, a little paranormal romance. I love to read this genre, and I thought it would be fun to write it. I touched on it with Mallory's story in Easy Magic, and I think you'll be pleased to see a glimpse of Mallory in this story as well.

Shadows is two years in the making. It seemed I always had other deadlines, other stories that came first. So when it was time to plot Shadows, and I sat down to write it, I was ecstatic.

And let me just tell you, it didn't disappoint.

I would like to point out that this story is darker than what I'm known for. The love story is there, of course, but there is also a quest involved that had me on the edge of my seat. Some of what's here may disturb you, as it should. We're talking about a serial killer, after all.

I hope you enjoy these sisters, their gifts, and the men who love them. This is the first of three books.

So sit back, make sure the lights are on, and let me tell you a story...

Kristen

PROLOGUE

Brielle

"Don't touch that!"

Daphne, my youngest sister, recoils from the rocking chair in the corner. It's dark under the stairs, but I know it's there.

I can see the shadow sitting in it.

The shadows are everywhere.

"Come on," I continue, gesturing for my sisters to huddle under our blanket fort with me. Shut out the shadows. The noises.

The house.

"I don't like it under here," Millie, the middle daughter says. She points her flashlight away from her face, illuminating our little haven, reflecting the quilt above us and casting everything in a red glow. We managed to sneak lots of pillows and old, ratty blankets under here. There's a storm raging tonight, and that's when it seems to be the worst.

For all of us.

We're what they call *sensitive*.

I've read books that I keep at school so our daddy doesn't see. It makes him the maddest of all.

And when Daddy's mad, we get punished.

I'm the oldest. At thirteen, I'm the one who protects my sisters from the house. From all of the bad things around us. It's always been this way. Our parents don't know. And even if they did, I'm not sure they'd care. Not really.

Because they don't believe me when I tell them about the shadows in the house.

And they don't believe Daphne when she says she sees things when she touches the old furniture.

A clap of thunder rocks the house, and Daphne lays her head in my lap, whimpering.

"I hope we don't get caught," Millie whispers. "Last time—"

"We won't," I assure. "Dad's not here, and Mama's passed out."

But, suddenly, there's a loud banging on the back door, and we all stare at each other in horror.

That entrance is only a few feet from where we're huddled under the stairs.

"She won't wake up," I whisper and pull Millie into my arms. "Please don't let her wake up."

But she does.

A few seconds later, we hear loud footsteps stomping through the house.

"I'm comin' already!" Mama yells to whoever's pounding on the door.

Soundlessly, we turn off our flashlights. Being in the dark is its own horrible torture.

But getting caught?

I don't want to even think it.

"What are you doin' here?" Mama demands after yanking open the front entry. I can feel the whoosh of air slide under the thin door of our hiding spot.

"Checkin' on you," a man says. "Storm's a doozy."

"We're fine," Mama replies. "You woke me out of a dead sleep."

"Where is he?" the man asks. I'm pretty sure it's Horace. He lives nearby and helps Mama and Daddy with things around the house.

"Gone," Mama says. "And he ain't comin' back."

I feel Daphne stiffen.

He's not coming back?

"That means you and me can—"

"It don't mean nothin'," Mama interrupts him. "Now, git. Git outta here, 'fore'n I sic the cops on you."

There are no more voices. Just a slamming door, and then Mama's feet stomping back down the hall and up the stairs to her bedroom. I hear the floorboards creak as she gets back into bed.

"Can we turn the light back on?" Millie whispers.

"Not yet," I mutter back to her. I need to make sure Mama's asleep before we turn on the lights or make any noise.

We're not supposed to be under here.

But it's the safest place in the house.

We're quiet for a long time. I run my fingers through Daphne's hair as she lays on my lap. Millie rests her head on my shoulder.

Our arms are looped around each other as the storm rages, and the house settles—more alive than ever.

"Do you hear it?" Millie asks.

The chair is rocking in the corner now, squeaking with every back and forth motion.

Footsteps upstairs. And they aren't Mama's.

"Can you tell if she's asleep?" I ask Millie.

"I don't want to reach out," she admits. Millie's psychic abilities are off the charts, even for a ten-year-old.

"Just real fast, then shut it down."

She sighs next to me and then is quiet while her mind searches the house.

"She's asleep," she whispers. "And he's here."

"Who?"

She whimpers. Daphne stirs and sits up.

"I saw him," Daphne says. "In my dream."

"Who?" I ask again and flip on my flashlight.

I don't have to ask a third time.

A new shadow is suddenly sitting with us.

"Daddy."

CHAPTER ONE

Brielle

"Hello, everyone, and welcome to my tour. I'm Brielle Landry, and I'll be your guide today. Now, I know there are roughly eleven thousand ghost tours in the French Quarter, so I thank you kindly for choosing mine."

I smile at the crowd that's gathered on the sidewalk before me. We have a group of all ages this evening, from young teenagers to middle-aged folks. There are those who want to be in the front, listening raptly. And then, of course, there are the drunk ones, who will likely be the hecklers.

"I have just a couple rules for y'all. No walking in the street. If you've been here for twenty minutes, you've already learned that drivers don't slow down, and I won't lose anyone to vehicular homicide on my tour."

The group laughs, and I continue, my eyes roaming the crowd and taking stock.

"We won't be going inside any of the beautiful buildings we'll be talking about tonight, but halfway through, we will stop at a bar to soak in some A/C and have a refreshment or two."

"Or five," Heckler Number One says, elbowing his friend.

"I'm always happy to answer questions, so don't be shy, y'hear? Now, let's get started."

I point to the big, gray building behind me. Most tours save this one for last, but not me. It's the most haunted of the group, and I want to get it over with.

Not that the rest of the tour *isn't* haunted. Ghosts are literally everywhere.

But this one? It's sinister.

I hate it.

Tour groups love it.

"This building behind me is the LaLaurie mansion," I begin. "Well, a rebuilt version of the original house, anyway. Like most buildings in the Quarter, it suffered a nasty fire. Delphine LaLaurie lived here with her third husband, Louis. She had two daughters from previous marriages. Both of her earlier husbands died early deaths."

I swallow hard as I look over at the façade. More shadows than I can count stare back at me.

"Delphine and Louis had a love for torture." The drama is thick in my New Orleans accent as I relay stories of torment, and the horrific atrocities done to the hundreds of slaves that once lived in the building behind me. "And these stories I just shared are the less horrible ones."

Several pairs of eyes whip to mine in surprise.

Including a pair of green orbs the same color as the malachite pendant I wear around my neck for protection.

I instinctively reach up and fiddle with the stone as I continue.

"Who haunts it?" someone calls out.

Who doesn't?

"One day, Delphine chased a twelve-year-old slave girl up to the roof of the building with a bullwhip. The young girl had been brushing Delphine's hair and hit a snag. She ran from the whip, and it's said she jumped to her death out of fear.

"Leah, the slave girl, is buried on the grounds of the mansion, along with countless others. When renovations were done years after Delphine and Louis fled to Paris, skeletons were found in the walls. So much death has happened here, that it wouldn't surprise me if dozens of spirits haunt the house.

"It was once owned by Nicolas Cage, but it has a different owner now. They don't offer tours."

I gesture for the group to follow me, and we continue down Royal Street.

My route through the Quarter is deliberate. I take the same path every day. There are no surprises that way.

Surprises for me are never fun.

Yes, I see shadows, but they're the same ones every time. I know where they lurk.

My hecklers turn out to be fun rather than ruining the tour for everyone else, and before long, we've stopped for our refreshments. I grab myself two bottles of water, one to drink now, and one to stow away in my bag for later.

"How do you know all this stuff?"

I turn and see those green eyes from before smiling down at me.

"I studied," I say with a grin of my own. The man is handsome as all get out, with a dimple in a cheek covered by dark stubble. But it's those eyes that draw me in. "I was a history major in college, and since I'm from this area, I've always been fascinated by local history."

"You tell a hell of a story."

"Thank you." I take a sip of my water, watching him. "Where are you from?"

"Savannah, originally."

"Another haunted city."

"They claim to be the most haunted in America."

I feel my smile turn colder. "While I've never been there, I'm sure Savannah is beautiful. But we have more dead in New Orleans than we have living. And while it's not a competition, I'd bet this city would stand up to yours any day of the week. At least, for hauntings."

"Maybe you need to visit."

Not a chance in hell.

"Maybe one day."

"I'm Cash." He holds out his hand to shake mine. His palm is warm, his grip strong.

"Brielle. But you knew that."

"You're a beautiful woman, Brielle."

"A complicated one." I wink at him, pull my hand away, and round up the troops. "Let's go, everyone. It's time for more ghost walking."

Once we're back on the sidewalk, I point to the building behind me. "This was once a boys' school. The original building burned down in the seventeen hundreds, and the boys perished in the building. It's said they still live here."

I glance back and see several small shadows looking out the windows.

"It's a hotel now, and guests have reported hearing laughter and children playing. Do you remember back in the day when we had regular film cameras?"

The older members of my group smile and nod.

"Well, back then, people would take their vacation photos. When they got home, they'd take the film in to be developed. Several vacationers reported that as they were sifting through their memories, they saw photos of them. Asleep. From above."

I glance over to see Cash raise one dark eyebrow. His dimple winks at me as he crosses his arms over his impressive chest and listens intently.

He would be less distracting if he were in the back of the group.

"So, while harmless, the boys *are* mischievous. They like to turn the channels on the TV."

"We're staying there." A woman looks up at her husband. "I'll never sleep tonight."

I laugh and, just as I turn to lead the group to the next point of interest, I falter and stop in my tracks.

A new shadow.

A new *shadow.*

About my height, standing on the sidewalk. I can never make out faces, but I can tell this one is turned toward me. It's a feminine spirit.

I blink quickly and try to recover so I don't alert my group to anything amiss.

A new shadow.

It's rare, even in the Quarter.

But I clear my throat and walk past the shadow to our next stop.

"THAT WAS *AMAZING*." A college-age girl smiles broadly and bounces on the balls of her feet. The tour ended fifteen minutes ago, but I always stay after to answer questions. "I'm Tammy. I just *loved* all of the stories. It's so interesting."

"I'm glad you enjoyed it."

"I was wondering about that Laurie house?"

"The LaLaurie?"

"Yeah. That one. Where can I learn more about her?

I mean, I know it sounds sick, but I'm fascinated by that stuff."

"Torture?"

She blushes. "History stuff. I guess it does sound awful, doesn't it?"

"There are lots of articles about Delphine online. Just Google the name, and you'll have more information than you can read. But I'll warn you, it's graphic."

"Thanks." She smiles at me, then hurries to catch up with her friend.

"People are morbidly curious," Cash says, joining me. He hung back, waiting for everyone else to ask their questions. Now, it's just the two of us.

"Always." I shudder. I know exactly what was done to those slaves.

Sometimes, the shadows talk.

"Did you have more questions, Cash?"

"One." I start to walk down the sidewalk, and he joins me. I expect him to ask about places that I didn't cover in my tour. Or maybe about the cemeteries.

Everyone always wants to know about those.

But I can't do tours there. It's too much.

Although I do have companies I can refer him to.

"What did you see?"

I stop and frown up at him. Cash is tall. Way taller than my five-foot-six height.

"Excuse me?"

"After you told the story about the kids dying in the fire, which is creepy as hell by the way, you turned, and then you stopped and went white as a sheet. You looked like you saw a ghost."

Well, I did see a ghost, Cash.

But I can't say that.

"It was great having you on the tour this evening." I smile at him and pat him on the arm. "Have a fantastic vacation. Be careful."

And with that, I hurry away, headed to the one place in the city that I'm absolutely safe.

"HELP ME PUT these chairs up, will you?"

Millie flutters around her little café, stacking chairs on tables so her night crew can come in and mop the floors.

Witches Brew will be three years old this spring, and so far, it's been a success for my younger sister. And it should be. This café is perfect for the French Quarter, from its fun name to the quirky décor and delicious menu.

Coffee served in a cauldron? Sure thing.

Want a love potion? You can order one up.

She'll also read your tarot cards if you ask nicely.

I know that tourists come in here and think it's just a fun, silly café.

But it's as real as it gets.

Millie is a gifted witch. A crazy, amazing psychic. And those love potions? Well, they're real.

She's a hedgewitch.

Or, in layman's terms, a kitchen witch.

And she's as scatterbrained and fun as she is a little scary.

I couldn't love her more.

"Whatcha doin'?" she asks as we place the chairs on the little, round tables.

"Just finished a tour. Figured I'd come in and see how business was today."

"Off the hook," she says and wipes the sweat off her brow with a towel. "And we're not even in the full swing of tourist season yet."

"Same." I smile at her. We're as different as can be. I'm dark-haired with blue eyes, and Millie is blond, tall, and has chocolate-brown eyes.

She's stunning.

"How many men did you have to chase out of here today?"

"Only one," she says, grinning. "If they'd stop ordering the love potion, I wouldn't have to chase them out at all."

"You know, you don't have to actually *give* them the potion every time. They'd never know the difference."

"I charge an extra three dollars for that brew," she says, raising her chin in the air. "And *I* would know the difference. I just need to remember to tell them not to drink it until they're outside."

I laugh and walk behind the counter that's lined with stools to help her fill the napkin dispensers.

"Aren't you exhausted?" Millie asks. "Why aren't you headed home?"

Because I saw a new shadow, and it freaked me out.

"Because I wanted to see my little sister."

"Uh-huh." She watches me closely. "I'm psychic, you know."

"You can't read me."

It's true. She can't. I have my shields up, and I'm shut down so tightly, there's no way she can read my mind. If I don't guard myself, I get inundated with spirits. Once upon a time, I thought I could escape it by moving somewhere else.

Two months in Colorado Springs proved that isn't true.

So, I came home and learned to build my walls and protect myself. Millie gave me the malachite.

So far, it's all working.

But I still see them.

"I met a guy tonight," I say casually.

"Spill it."

"His name is Cash." I wrinkle my nose. "I mean, who names their kid *Cash*?"

"Is he hot?"

"Yeah. Tall, dark, and handsome, with green eyes."

"Nice. Did he ask for your number?"

"No."

She sticks out her bottom lip in disappointment.

"He might have, but I blew him off before he could."

"Wait." She holds up a hand, her bracelets jangling. "Why would you do that?"

I take a deep breath and round the counter so I can sit on a stool. "Because he noticed something."

She raises a brow.

"I was finishing up at the Andrew Jackson Hotel."

She nods.

"As I was about to walk down the street, I turned, and there was a shadow on the sidewalk. Just standing there. I've never seen her before."

"*Her?*"

"Yeah, she was about my height. Very feminine."

"Did she say anything?"

"Not that I heard. It just threw me because you know how careful I am about my route. I don't like surprises, especially not like this. It's creepy as hell. And, yes, I know I should be used to it by now, but—"

"It's creepy, like you said." She leans on the counter and bites her lip, thinking. "It probably means that someone recently died there."

"I know that."

"And now it's a new spirit on your tour. Too bad she didn't say anything. If she did, you could add it to your show. Could be fun. *Lucy was killed in this building three days ago, and her spirit now wanders the sidewalk in front of her former home.*"

"Talk about creepy."

I sigh and run my fingers through my hair. "Did you sweep this area recently?"

"Is the floor dirty?"

I look at her as if she's being obtuse on purpose. "You know what I mean."

"It's been about a week."

"You need to do it again."

Millie frowns, looking around the space. Her shields are as strong as mine, maybe stronger because she doesn't just see the dead, she *feels* them, and that's much more dangerous.

She fiddles with the amethyst around her neck.

"What do you see?"

I narrow my eyes. "I shouldn't tell you."

"I don't want to look, Bri. I dropped my guard for just a second earlier and was slammed with the pervy thoughts of a nineteen-year-old college kid who couldn't take his eyes off my ass. So, just tell me. Is it the little girl again?"

"Yeah. And she brought a friend." I reach over to take my sister's hand. "Don't drop your shields anymore, Mill. Not for a minute. *Ever.* I know we live and work here in the Quarter because it's where we make our living, but it could really hurt us."

"I know."

"I couldn't bear it if I lost you, too."

She shakes her head. "You didn't lose Daphne."

"She's not speaking to me."

"Because you're both stubborn as hell, and you need to get over it."

"You always were the peacekeeper."

"That's what being the middle child does for you, it literally puts you in the middle. I love you both. Now, snap out of it and just call her."

"I will."

"Liar."

I laugh and then frown when a third shadow appears. It looks just like the one from the sidewalk.

"What is it?"

"You need to cleanse this place. I think all of the different auras coming in and out of here all day is leaving some residual energy behind."

"I'll do it tonight before I leave. I'm also going to make you something special, so don't move that butt from that seat."

"You're bossy."

"And sassy." She winks as she fills a stainless-steel shaker with all kinds of things that I don't recognize.

This is not my area of expertise.

I can talk about the history of New Orleans all day.

My sister, however, mixes potions and casts spells.

She's gifted. She learned with some of the most powerful witches in the world, right here in New Orleans.

"How is Miss Sophia?" I ask, making Millie smile.

"She's amazing. She said to tell you hello. And to guard yourself." Millie frowns. "I forgot to pass that along. But she also said that you need to be strong regarding what's to come."

"What's that mean? What's coming?"

"She didn't say."

"She always leaves the most important parts out."

Millie pours the concoction into a glass and slides it over to me.

"No love potion, right?"

"No. It's a shielding potion. For protection."

I sniff it. "Smells like strawberries." I take a sip and smile in surprise. "Wow, it's like a milkshake."

"Helps it go down easier," she says with a wink. "Come back tomorrow, and I'll make you another."

"I'll gain ten pounds." I take another sip. "But I don't think I care. Wait, can you just do some kind of spell to take the calories out?"

"Sorry." She giggles and drinks the rest of the drink herself. "If I could do that, I'd be super-rich."

I finish my drink, and after I help Millie wash my glass and tidy up from the impromptu beverage, I wave goodbye to her.

"Be careful," she says before closing the door.

I'm always careful.

I take the same path from her place to mine, every single time. So far, I haven't seen any shadows on this route, and that makes me happy. The bars and clubs are hopping, full of tourists drinking and dancing. The French Quarter hums with energy, no matter the time of day.

I glance to my right just before I cross the street that leads several more blocks to where my apartment is, and am surprised to see Cash standing on the sidewalk, leaning against a pole.

"Are you following me?" I ask.

"No, ma'am," he says with an easy smile. "It seems I'm just destined to run into you. Can't say that I mind."

I smile back at him, regretting the way I brushed him off earlier.

"Well, then, perhaps I'll run into you again."

"I do hope so." He winks, and I hurry along to my apartment.

I round the corner of my block and stop in my tracks.

"Who are you?"

There's no answer, but I know it's the same shadow from the sidewalk and from Millie's café.

No shadows have ever followed me before.

Why now?

CHAPTER TWO

"Where do you think you're going?"

~Ted Bundy

She's perfect.

He's been looking for the right one. It's been a few weeks since he last took someone, and he finally got rid of that toy this morning. Having just one subject at a time isn't really his style.

He likes having several girls in his lair at once. They talk to each other. They conspire. Hearing their chorus of pleas, their cries, gives him great joy. It arouses him far more than sex ever could. Women aren't to be used as sexual partners.

They're his prey.

They think they can escape him. Go back to their pathetic little lives.

Why are women so fucking stupid? Don't they know he has something far better waiting for them?

He grins as he watches from his usual spot under the streetlight. His shoulder leans against the pole as he watches Brielle finish up her nightly tour.

He comes every night.

She's never seen him.

He'll have to teach her to be more careful. More watchful. Bad things could happen to her, and he needs her whole, so she's hale and hearty and ready for what he has planned for her.

But that's for later. Right now, he needs someone new. Someone fresh.

And he's looking right at her.

"I'm Tammy. I just *loved* all of the stories. It's so fascinating."

Well, hello, Tammy.

She could be a mirror image of Brielle.

And that just can't be, can it?

Brielle finishes talking with Tammy, then moves to take more questions. He approaches the young woman.

"I just heard you ask about the LaLaurie mansion."

She turns to him with wide, blue eyes. Oh, yes, she's perfect. Those eyes with the dark hair. She's the right height, too.

Tonight's going to be fun.

"Yes, do you know more?" she asks.

"I know plenty, and I have a friend who can give us a private tour," he replies kindly. "In fact, we can go back there now, if you like."

"Oh, I don't know," Tammy says, looking around. "I came with friends, and they'll be pissed if I ditch them."

"You'll be back here before you know it," he lies easily. "Don't you worry."

She bites her lip, considering her options, but curiosity gets the best of her, and she nods.

"All right, then. But I have to hurry."

"No problem. Come with me."

He's always calm, and this is no different. He guides her through the crowds of the French Quarter and down the street toward the house she's so interested in.

But instead of approaching the door to knock, he turns to his car.

"Aren't we going inside?"

"I just have to call first since they're not expecting me."

"Oh, right." She offers him a tentative smile and nods. "That makes sense."

He can see the nerves starting to set in. She's wondering if she made the right choice.

Before she can flee, he reaches for the syringe he has ready, resting in the cupholder of the front seat. She doesn't see it coming when he turns swiftly and jabs the needle into her arm. Within seconds, she's drooping against him.

"Too much to drink tonight, darlin'," he says with a smile and guides her into the backseat. "Let's go sober you up. You don't want to miss the fun."

CHAPTER THREE
Cash

"I'm going to gain about sixty pounds while I'm here." I lean back in my chair and rub my flat stomach. "You keep bringing me to amazing restaurants."

"Would you rather we take you to crappy ones?" my brother, Andrew, asks with a grin.

"Touché." I take a sip of my water and blink rapidly when I see Brielle walk through the door.

"What?" Andy's wife, Felicia, says and turns to see what I'm looking at. "Do you know her?"

"Sort of."

I grin when Brielle's eyes scan the room and then catch mine. Recognition sparks, and then pleasure moves over her beautiful face.

I'm embarrassed to admit that I'm relieved.

If she'd been disgusted and turned to leave, my ego would have taken a hard hit.

"Are you following me?" I ask her when she walks up to our table.

"I could say the same thing for you, Mr. Stalker," she says, grinning, and turns to my family. "Hi. I'm Brielle."

"This is my brother Andy, and his wife, Felicia."

"Pleasure," Brielle says and nods. "I see you found my favorite restaurant in the Quarter."

"It's ours, too," Felicia says. "Would you like to join us?"

"Join us," I agree, gesturing to the chair next to me.

"Oh, thanks for the invitation, but you've finished your meal, and I ordered mine to go." She winks at me, and I feel it all the way to my gut. She pats my shoulder. "Y'all have a good day."

She walks away to collect her meal from the counter and then sashays out of the restaurant and down the street.

"How do you know her?" Felicia asks. She leans in, avidly awaiting every detail.

Felicia is a busy-body from way back.

"I don't know her well," I reply. "She was the guide on the ghost tour I took the other night. You know, when you guys ditched me for date night, and I had to fend for myself?"

"You went on a *ghost tour*?" Felicia's eyes dance with excitement. "How was it?"

"Interesting, actually." I sip my water again. "She has a way with telling a story, that's for sure."

"And, at the risk of getting slapped by my gorgeous wife, she's not bad on the eyes," Andy adds.

"She's beautiful," Felicia agrees, nodding. "You should ask her out."

"She might not be single."

"No ring," Felicia says immediately. "Trust me, girls look for that stuff."

"That doesn't mean she's not—"

"He might never see her again," Andy adds.

"I want to go on a ghost tour," Felicia announces. "I've always wanted to do it but never made the time. We've lived here for two whole years, babe. It's time we go."

"It just so happens, I know a guide," I say with a grin, the idea of seeing Brielle again sparking immediate joy.

"That's handy."

We both look at Andy, who just sighs. "Fine. I'm in. But I don't believe in any of that haunting, ghostly, voodoo shit."

"So noted," I reply.

"And after the tour, Cash should ask Brielle on a date."

"Wait, what?"

Felicia claps her hands. "It's perfect. It can't hurt to *ask*. If she's taken, she'll say so. No harm, no foul. But she was looking at you with interest, brother mine."

"She won't stop nagging until you ask the hot girl out," Andy says. "So, just save us both the headache."

"I love you, too."

Andy grins. "Let's go ghost hunting."

"THANKS FOR COMING on the tour with me this evening, everyone," Brielle says, smiling at the group. It's a larger one than the other night. "I'll hang around in case anyone has any questions. No pressure, though. Have a good night."

"Now," Felicia says in a loud whisper. "Go ask her now."

"You're pushy," I say calmly and watch as several people huddle around the gorgeous brunette to ask their questions. "I'll let the others talk with her first."

"Smart," Andy says on a yawn. "But I'm not waiting around. Let's go home, babe."

"I want to see Cash ask her out," Felicia says, frowning. "This is the best part, and that's saying a lot because that tour was *awesome*. I wonder if our house is haunted."

"Let's go see," Andy says with a wink. "Give the man some space. It's creepy to hover when he's about to make his move."

"Is it creepy?" she asks me.

"No, I don't think you're creepy, but you guys go ahead. I don't know how long she'll be."

Felicia's hopeful expression falls, but she nods. "Okay. But I want all of the details later."

"Of course, you do." I laugh as I wave them off, then turn to listen as Brielle talks about other legends and ghosts in the French Quarter.

"Thanks for your time," an older blonde says with a smile before walking away and leaving Brielle alone.

"So...I swear I'm not a stalker," I say as I approach her. She turns and smiles at me, but it doesn't reach her eyes. The carefree woman from earlier is gone.

Suddenly, I want to scoop her into my arms and protect her.

And she hasn't even said that anything is wrong.

"I was surprised to see the three of you join the tour tonight," she admits.

"After you left the restaurant this afternoon, Felicia announced that she'd always wanted to go on a ghost tour. She talked us into coming."

"I hope she had a good time."

"She did." I shift from foot to foot, suddenly nervous.

And I'm never nervous.

"I have a question."

"Sure."

"Are you involved with anyone? Husband? Boyfriend?"

The smile reaches her eyes now. "No. I'm not involved with anyone."

"Well, that's good, because I'd like to ask you out for some coffee."

"Right now?"

I glance around and then turn back to her. "Sure. If you're free."

"Have you been to Café du Monde yet?"

"I can't say that I have."

She smiles and motions for me to walk with her. "Then you're in for a treat. The fastest route is through Jackson Square, but I'd like to go another way if that's okay."

"Is it so you have more time with me? It's all right, you can admit it."

She laughs loudly. When I take her hand in mine, she doesn't pull away. "I just have certain routes that I prefer to take through the city. It's an OCD thing. A quirk, if you will."

"I don't mind quirks that keep me in your company."

We're quiet as she leads me down the dark streets full of loud people. Music pours from the doors of bars and restaurants. It's a symphony of noise.

Even if I wanted to chat with her, it would be difficult. But I'm fine just walking together, holding her hand.

I can't explain it. I barely know her, but I crave her company.

It was as if I recognized her the second I saw her.

With my background in psychology, I could probably tear into the whys and hows of that and make it incredibly *not* romantic.

Or, I could just enjoy it. Relax.

That's what I'm supposed to be doing in New Orleans anyway.

"It's just down here," she says loudly, pointing to the end of the block. She leads me to the front of the line, and we're offered a little, round table that has a napkin dispenser on it and nothing else. "The menu is here."

She points to the side of the dispenser.

"But, if you trust me, I'll order for us. Just tell me if you want hot or cold coffee."

I cock a brow, watching as she tucks a dark strand of hair behind her ear. "Cold."

She nods, and a woman approaches to take our order.

"We'll have two frozen café au laits, and a family order of beignets," Brielle says. I pay for the order, and the woman hurries off to fill it.

"So, tell me more about you," I say.

"Actually," Brielle says, crossing her legs and watching me closely, "why don't you tell me about *you*? All I know is your name. Cash. Is that short for something?"

"It's short for Cassien. What else would you like to know? You know I'm from Savannah."

"What do you do for work?"

I fidget in my seat. "I work for the FBI."

Her brows lift. "You're an FBI agent?"

"I am." I nod and lean back when two frozen drinks and a large plate of beignets are set before us. "I've been with them for about ten years."

"What do you do for them?"

"I'm a profiler."

"Wow, that's fascinating," she says and takes a bite of a donut. "Do you profile murderers? Like serial killers?"

"Sometimes." I nod and watch as she licks some powdered sugar from her lower lip.

I want to lick that lip myself.

"Okay, that's pretty cool, Cash. I can honestly say I've never met a profiler before."

"That you know of."

She nods. "True. Do you work out of Savannah?"

"I'm actually based in the Dallas field office, but I travel frequently, going wherever I'm needed."

"And what are you doing in New Orleans?"

I sigh and suddenly wish the coffee were whiskey.

"I'm on mandatory leave."

She tips her head to the side. "Did you kill someone in the line of duty?"

"No." Not this time. "I just came off a pretty intense case. I haven't taken a vacation in a long time, and my boss pretty much pushed me out the door. I'm not welcome back for a few weeks."

"That's quite a vacation."

"Too long." I sigh, still frustrated. "I'm not used to being idle. That's how I found you. Andy and Felicia wanted to go out on a date the other night, and I didn't want to sit at their place alone, so I went out and found your tour."

"I'm glad you did," she says quietly. "Is it weird that

I feel like I've met you before? I barely know you. You're a stranger. Yet, here I am, hanging out with you like we're old friends."

"It's not weird, I was just thinking the same. Maybe we met in a former life or something."

She doesn't laugh at that. She just narrows her eyes and taps her lips, seeming to give it some thought.

"I was joking."

"I know you were, but I suppose it's possible."

"Do you believe in past lives?"

Her eyes meet mine. "I believe in a lot of things, Cash. And I'm going to tell you, right here and now, even when I barely know you, that if you'd like for us to simply go our separate ways, I won't hold it against you."

I frown. "That feels a little dramatic."

"It's not." She wipes her hands, finishing the last of her treat. "I told you the other night, I'm a complicated woman. I wasn't kidding."

"I suppose we're all complicated, in our own ways. You haven't scared me off."

"Yet," she whispers.

"Okay, tell me what you think would send me running?"

"I see dead people," she says with a straight face. "It's why I'm so good at my job. I don't just know the lore because I studied it. Much of what I know has been told to me by the souls who experienced it themselves."

I blink at her. I honestly don't know what to say.

"See? Complicated."

"How long has it been that way for you?"

"Since my earliest memories," she says. "And, yes, it's scary. I don't know if I'll ever get used to it entirely, but I've learned to live with it."

"Being in the French Quarter must be unbearable for you."

She tips her head to the side. "Huh. You haven't run off yet."

"I see no reason to go anywhere."

"To answer your question, no, the Quarter isn't super fun for someone like me. But I make my living here. And I take precautions."

"What kind of precautions?"

"I think I've talked about myself long enough. Tell me more about you. Why the FBI?"

"Well, I got my Ph.D. in psychology and then decided to go through the academy. I always knew I wanted to work for the FBI. Maybe I read too many thrillers when I was a kid. It was a lot of studying and training. As I mentioned, I've been an agent for about ten years, and a profiler for five, meaning post-training."

"Good for you. Do you enjoy it?"

"Despite some of the things I've seen, you mean? Yes. Because, at the end of the day, we put monsters in cages."

"I bet you've seen a lot of horrible stuff."

More horrible than you can imagine.

"You said you're originally from the area?" I ask, changing the subject. She smiles and stands, motioning for me to follow her.

"I'll tell you about my sordid past while you walk me home."

"Deal."

"I grew up out in the bayou, about an hour from the city. I have two sisters, both younger. My parents were pathetic and horrible excuses for human beings."

"That good, huh?"

"Abusive." She shrugs one shoulder, and I feel immediate and intense anger. I want to hurt anyone who would dare abuse this woman. "Neglect. Not to mention, we lived in the most haunted house in Louisiana, and that's saying a lot."

"Wow."

"Do *you* believe in ghosts, Cash?"

I frown, thinking it over. "I think I like a good story. But I don't know if I believe, to be honest, because I've never experienced anything paranormal."

"Never?"

"Not that I'm aware of. I know I've never seen a ghost."

"Have you ever been somewhere and, suddenly, all of the hairs on your body stand on end, and you don't know why?"

"Sure."

"Or walked into a room that suddenly feels a lot colder than any other part of the house?"

"Everyone's felt a chill."

She smiles up at me. "You've experienced things, Cash. You just didn't know that you were experiencing them."

"Huh."

"Or are you one of those people who thinks things like this don't exist?"

"I've seen evil," I reply honestly. "And I'm not so close-minded that I can say there's not something out there that we can't see. I can't say I'm a believer, but I think *you* believe it, and sometimes, that's all that matters."

"That's a good answer."

"Do you live here in the Quarter?"

"Yes." She nods and leads me around a corner. "I have an apartment just down the street here."

"Is it haunted?"

"Everything's haunted. But the spirits there are calm and don't bother me much."

I take her hand once more, and when her fingers clench hard on mine, I frown down at her.

She stops short, staring straight ahead.

It's like watching her the other night all over again.

"Brielle? What's wrong?"

"This has never happened before," she whispers, and I can see she's starting to shake.

"Hey. Hey." I tip her face up to mine. "I'm right here, and I won't let anything hurt you. But you have to tell me what's happening."

"We have to go inside," she says. "Will you come with me?"

"Of course."

She's walking fast now, almost pulling me along the sidewalk. She turns to the side as if she's slinking past something she doesn't want to touch, then hurries up the stairs to her apartment.

She fumbles with the lock, so I take the key from her, unlock the door, and walk in with her. She immediately slams the door, leans against it, and looks up at me with round, glassy eyes.

"*Now* you're scaring me," I inform her.

"I need my sister," she says, pulling her phone out of her pocket. "I'm going to call for her, and while she's on her way, I'll tell you everything."

"Deal."

Her eyes are on mine as she holds the phone to her ear. "It's me. I need you right now. I'm at home. Okay, but Cash is here, and I haven't told him yet. See you soon."

She hangs up, but instead of talking, she just walks right into my arms and hugs me tightly as if she's holding on for dear life.

As if she's pulling strength from me.

"Brielle," I whisper and kiss the top of her head. She smells like lavender. "Talk to me."

She pulls back and paces to the window, staring down at the street. "She's still there. Both of them are."

"Who? I didn't see anyone."

"I can't be sure who the first one is," she says and turns to me. "But the other one? It's Tammy. From my tour the other night.

"She's dead."

CHAPTER FOUR

Brielle

I can't find my center.

Hell, I can barely breathe.

This hasn't happened since I was a child.

"Talk to me, Brielle," Cash says. His hands are strong on my shoulders, his green eyes concerned but not disgusted.

"Like I said earlier, if you want to go, I understand. Because it's about to get weird, Cash. I wish I was like normal girls, but I'm not, and I'm telling you now, you should probably go."

"I'm not going anywhere."

I swallow hard, fighting back tears of relief and joy. If one of my sisters told me that they already trusted their life with a man they only met days ago, I'd tell them they were nuts.

But here we are. I can't explain why or even how, but

I *know* him already. I can feel it down in my bones that I can trust him—with even my deepest secrets.

"I told you, I see dead people."

"Let's sit."

"No, I'd prefer to stand. I need to pace a bit." I walk away and look out the window again.

No shadows.

Apparitions.

"I always see shadows," I continue. "I've never been able to make out the features of the spirits I see, though."

"Until now?" He guesses correctly.

"Until now," I confirm. "And let me just say, it'll scare the hell out of a girl."

"I can only imagine."

There's a knock on the door, startling us both.

"It's me!" Millie yells through the door, and I rush over to open it. "What's wrong? Wait. Hi, I'm Millie."

She holds out her hand for Cash to shake, which he does immediately.

"Cash."

"I know." Her eyes narrow as she examines him, and I know she's sweeping his thoughts. It's intrusive as all get out, but she's my sister, and that makes her protective. "I like you."

"I feel like I was just given a test that I didn't prepare for."

"You were," Millie confirms. "You passed. Now,"—she turns to me again—"talk to me."

"So, I saw that new shadow the other night."

Millie nods.

"Well, just before I called you, I saw something else that's new. Not just a new shadow. An apparition."

She blinks rapidly. "As in, you saw their *features*?"

"Yes." I nod and then start pacing the living area again. "For both of them. The first one, the one I saw the other night, isn't a shadow anymore. Now, there are *two*. Girls. And one is from my tour the night I met Cash."

Millie slowly lowers herself to the couch, perching on the edge of it, watching me with wide, brown eyes. "They must be trying to communicate with you."

"Their mouths were moving." It comes out as a whisper, and a shiver slithers down my spine. "But I couldn't hear what they were saying."

"Wait." Millie holds up her hand, her eyes wider than before. "This means they're *following* you, Bri."

"Yeah." I sigh and rub my fingertips over my forehead. "Yeah, that started the other night."

"You didn't say anything," Millie says.

"To either of us," Cash adds, his hands balling into fists at his sides.

"Well, to be fair, this is our first date," I remind him, but he doesn't laugh. He just narrows his eyes at me.

"It's a hell of a first date," Millie mumbles. "I mean, most people just get naked and have sex and then regret their life choices in the morning. This is on a whole different level."

I smirk and then shrug. "The night's not over yet."

"This isn't funny," Cash says, slowly shaking his head. "You're being terrorized by the dead, Brielle."

"Sometimes it's either laugh or cry, and I don't want to cry," I admit. "Trust me, I've cried over crap like this all my life."

"There has to be a way to shut it off," he mutters as if he's thinking aloud. "Hypnosis? It's not my area of expertise, but I have friends—"

"I'm thirty." I prop my hands on my hips. "Trust me, we've tried everything to at least tone it down. It just is what it is, and I've learned to deal with it. That's why I have certain routes I take through the Quarter. No surprises. I chose this apartment because the spirits here are quiet. I don't travel much. I have a routine, Cash, and it's worked well for me."

"Until today," Millie says softly. "We need to find out what these girls want and send them on their way so you can get back to a somewhat normal life again. You know what happened the last time."

"Wait, this has happened before?" Cash demands. My eyes are pinned on my sister's.

"Not the apparitions. This is brand new," I reply. "But the following has happened before. I'll tell you about it later." I turn back to my sister. "I need for them to go away," I agree. "Because I'm afraid I can't give them what they want. Whatever it is they need."

"We don't know if we don't know," Millie says. "I can

open myself up and feel them for you if you want, since you can't hear them."

"No," I say immediately, rushing to her and taking her shoulders in my hands. "Do *not* do that, Millicent. I'm not giving you permission to do that."

"Okay, I won't."

"Promise me."

"I promise."

"I'm missing something."

We both turn to Cash, who watches us intently.

"If she opens herself up and crawls into the mind of a spirit, there's a good chance she won't walk back out again," I inform him. "Millie is a powerful psychic."

"I'm a witch, too," she says proudly.

"Does everyone in the family have these,"—he waves his hand in the air—"gifts?"

"Just the sisters," I reply. "Daphne is the youngest, and she's psychometric. She touches objects and sees the past through them."

"Fascinating," he says.

"Honestly, I'm shocked he hasn't run away screaming yet," Millie says to me. "Or called the cops."

"He *is* the cops," I say with a shrug. "FBI profiler."

"A *profiler?*" She stands and walks to him. "So, you're a psychiatrist?

"I am," he confirms.

"May I?"

"Sure."

She takes his hand, looks deeply into his eyes, and

after about fifteen seconds, leans in to give him a gentle hug.

"I'm so sorry."

"It's okay." He hugs her in return and smiles when she pulls away. "I'm not running, Millie. I'm confused, intrigued, and completely entranced by your sister. I'm worried, as well. And, frankly, I want to hurt anyone that would even dare to try and hurt *her*."

"Really like him," Millie says to me with a grin. "If you don't scoop him up, I will."

"He's not meant for you."

"No." She shakes her head. "No, he's not."

"So, what now?" Cash asks. "What do we do now?"

"There's nothing to do yet," I reply. "I freaked out a bit because this is all new, but we don't have anything to act on."

"Two women are dead," he reminds us. "We have to call the authorities and get an investigation underway. I have contacts here, I can call—"

"But we don't know the circumstances," Millie says, interrupting him. "They might have been in an accident together. They might have died of natural causes. They could have died years ago and are just now reaching out —though that doesn't make sense with you talking to the one girl the other night."

"We wait," I add, nodding. "And in the meantime, I'll just have two creepy girls following me around. Oh, and one more thing. They didn't die of natural causes, that much is clear."

No, the torture marks on their skin weren't anything *normal*.

They were killed; after they were put through inexplicable horrors.

"WAS THAT YOUR FIRST SAGE CLEANSING?" I ask after Millie leaves for the night. She stayed and helped me sweep my apartment for anything that made its way inside. It should also tone down the resident spirits for a while.

"It was," Cash says. He leans on my kitchen counter, watching as I tidy up, trying to keep my hands busy for a little while longer.

He's ridiculously handsome. Hot, even. Tall and broad with muscles and tanned skin. His lower front teeth are just a little crooked, which only makes his smile more interesting.

But I could get lost in those green eyes.

"What are you thinking?" he asks.

"That you should probably go. I've kept you here for far too long."

His eyes narrow on my face. "I'm not going anywhere."

"So, I know I joked around earlier about sex on the first date, but I'm not getting naked with you tonight. Sorry to disappoint."

"Funny." He chuckles and reaches out to drag his

knuckles down my cheek. "I'll sleep on the couch. I don't want to leave you alone tonight. What if they haunt your dreams?"

"Sleep's always been my safe place." I can't hold back from wrapping my arms around his middle and hugging him. "I appreciate you thinking of it, but I've never had sleeping issues, thank goodness."

"Well, that's something, then." He kisses the top of my head. "But I'm still staying. We've already established that, although this is new, it's strong. And if you think I won't be here to protect you, you still have a lot to learn about me."

"I don't think you can protect me against this," I whisper into his chest. "But having you here is soothing, so, thank you. You don't have to sleep on the couch. I have a guest bedroom. I don't get many visitors, but I have it anyway."

"I'll take it," he says. "Where's your room?"

"Second door on the right."

"Come on."

He takes my hand and leads me to my bedroom. He turns down the bed and then faces me. "I'll go make you some hot tea. Your sister pointed out the one I should use."

"She's helpful."

"You get ready for bed, and I'll be back in a few minutes."

"Cash." He stops in the doorway and turns back to me. "Thank you."

"You're welcome."

I can hear him puttering around in my kitchen as I change into yoga shorts and a loose tank top, then pad into the bathroom to brush my teeth and my long, dark hair. I wash my face, and just as I walk out of the bathroom, Cash walks into the bedroom with two steaming cups of tea.

"Thank you again," I say as I sit on the bed and accept a mug. "I'm glad you made yourself a cup. I was going to suggest it. It'll protect you, too."

"Am I in danger?"

I frown. "I don't think so. I know that nothing here can hurt you. Or would want to. Trust me, I wouldn't live here if that were the case. But, just in case, the tea can't hurt."

He nods and sits in the rocking chair across from the bed, watching me. His brow lifts when we hear footsteps in the living room.

"That's normal," I say with a grin. "It'll calm down in a few minutes."

"Do you just live your life in fear, every single day?" he asks, surprising me. I think back to the three of us huddled under the stairs of the god-awful house we grew up in.

"For a long time, we did. The three of us. Our childhood wasn't fantastic, Cash, and only half of that was due to our gifts and not understanding them. The other half was our parents."

"You mentioned them earlier."

"My father died when I was thirteen." I take a sip of tea and guard my mind, reinforcing my personal shields and grounding myself. He's been truly gone for a long time, but I don't want to take any chances. "I'm pretty sure my mother killed him, but I can't be sure."

"You're kidding."

"I wish I were." I shrug a shoulder. "He haunted the three of us for a decade. He's the only spirit that's ever followed me. Before this week. He was a bastard when he was living, punishing us for the smallest things. He took a lot of joy in inflicting pain."

"Fucking hell, Brielle."

"And it didn't stop after he died. So, yes, our childhood was full of fear. Then, once the three of us were all out of the house, Millie started studying with Miss Sophia, a very powerful witch, not far from our childhood home. She told her about our father, and Miss Sophia was finally able to create a spell to get rid of him forever. Without her help, I'm sure he'd still be around."

Cash's jaw clenches. "And your mother? Is she dead, too?"

"No." My smile turns cold. "But if I had my way, she would be."

"You can't tell an FBI agent that you wish your mother was dead."

"Yes, I can." I raise my chin. "While my father inflicted punishment and pain, she simply ignored it. Ignored *us*. I raised my sisters, not our parents. In fact, when I turned eighteen, I moved out and took them with me, filing for full custody. She didn't fight it. She still lives in that godsforsaken house in the bayou, by herself, slowly dying.

"She didn't believe us when we told her about what we saw, what we felt. And she would beat us with the belt if we talked about it."

"Christ."

"So, when we left, I immediately called other people in the area that were like us. And I started to ask questions. Built a community around us. We learned, we grew stronger, and after a while, we healed."

"I'm so glad. I hate that you went through that."

"Maybe we're all stronger because of it," I reply honestly. "We learned to control ourselves out of necessity, so our gifts aren't messy or frivolous now."

"That's a positive way to look at it."

He blinks slowly, watching me.

"What about your family? Tell me about them."

"Does it sound weird for me to say that I feel guilty that I had the exact opposite of you?"

"You shouldn't feel guilty at all."

"Andy is my only sibling. He's a couple of years younger than I am, and he works for the New Orleans PD."

"Lots of law enforcement in your family."

"My dad was a cop," he says and nods. "He was killed in the line of duty when I was eighteen."

"Oh, Cash. I'm sorry."

He nods and drinks the rest of his tea, then sets the

mug aside. "It was tough. Mom never remarried. She still lives in Savannah. She's been sick lately."

His eyes hold mine.

"Cancer."

"Why aren't you there with her?"

"I was," he says on a sigh. "I went there first, and she's doing much better. She basically shooed me out the door and told me to go spend some time with my brother."

"She sounds wonderful."

"She is," he says with a nod. "But, to be honest, I was ready to go. All she does is lecture me about working too hard, and that I need to find a nice girl to settle down with."

"She loves you." I set my empty mug aside and lie down, facing Cash. I pull the blankets up around my shoulders and smile at him. "I swear, it's not the company making me tired."

"You had a busy day," he says, letting out a small laugh. "And an emotional one. If you need me, I'll be next door, okay?"

"Okay."

He crosses to me and kisses my forehead, then turns off the light and leaves the door open just a crack. I hear him walk to the kitchen, set our empty mugs in the sink, and then into the guest room. His feet shuffle around as he gets ready for bed, then the bedsprings squeak a bit as he climbs under the covers. And then it's quiet. Even the spirits have settled down.

My eyes droop, and before long, I sink into sleep.

This is new. It seems today is the day for it, whether I'm awake or asleep.

Have I mentioned that I don't like surprises?

I'm walking through the Quarter on my usual route to work. I nod at people I know and ignore the shadows that lurk in the corners. I'm used to them. Some don't know I'm here, and some try to get my attention, but I always keep my eyes straight ahead.

Focus. Focus is always the key. Stay centered. Grounded. Keep my mind calm. If I let the fear sink in, I'll make myself vulnerable, and that's not good.

The sun is up and bright in the sky, but suddenly, a shadow covers it, sending everything into darkness. I stop and blink, trying to let my eyes adjust to the dim surroundings. When I can see at least some things again, they're right in front of me.

The two women.

The two apparitions that have been following me for days.

"You have to help us," Tammy, the one from my tour group says. "You have to find us."

"Find us," the other agrees. They reach out for me. Both are covered in blood, and wounds still seep all over their bodies. The girl I don't know has a slit throat, and one eye is missing.

Tammy doesn't have any fingers on her right hand.

"Who hurt you?" I ask, but no sound comes out of my mouth. "Tell me who hurt you."

"There are more," Tammy says. "So many more. We need you. You have to find us."

"Who did this?" I ask again, frustrated when no sound

emerges. Damn it! I need to communicate with them. "Please, tell me how to find you."

"*Help us,*" they say in unison. "*Please. You have to help us.*"

"Holy shit."

Suddenly, I'm sitting up in bed, gasping for air. Cash holds my shoulders firmly.

"Brielle, wake up. You're safe, baby. Wake up."

"I'm awake," I gasp and lean in to rest my forehead on his chest.

"You were having a nightmare."

"No." I look up into his green eyes. They seem brighter in the dim light. "I was dream-walking. The girls are talking, Cash."

"What did they say?"

"They asked me to help them. Find them." I feel a tear slide down my cheek. "Horrible things were done to them."

"They told you?"

"I could see it." I swallow hard. My mouth is so dry. "He tortured them."

"Where are they?"

"I don't know." I shake my head in despair. "I don't know."

CHAPTER FIVE

Brielle

"Good morning."

I smile at Cash as I walk into the living room and sit on the couch next to him. He passes me his coffee, and I take a sip.

"Good morning."

I think I could get used to having him here like this. After he comforted me in the middle of the night, he stayed with me, holding me until I fell back to sleep. And this morning, when I woke up, he was no longer in bed with me, but I could smell the coffee.

"How do you feel?"

"Tired." I shrug and take another sip of his coffee, then pass it back to him. "I guess dream-walking will do that to a person."

"You guess?"

"This week is full of firsts."

Cash frowns and takes my hand in his, linking our

fingers. "I'm worried about you, Brielle. And I barely know you."

"Thank you." I lean my head on the couch and watch him thoughtfully. "I'm seriously shocked that you haven't escaped yet. Why are you still here?"

He blows out a breath and sets his mug aside. "I was asking myself that this morning. It's not that I feel bad for you, or even that I feel an obligation."

"Good."

"I'm drawn to you in ways I can't explain. Like I said before, it's a...recognition. Like, I was looking for you and didn't even know it."

"Same," I whisper.

"I've never believed in soul mates or that sort of thing," he says. "And I'm not sure I do now. But there's something here, and I'm going to stay for as long as you'll let me."

I smile just as a knock comes from the front door.

"Are you expecting someone?" Cash asks.

"It's probably Millie." I walk to the entry and look out the peephole, then open the door and smile at my sister. "I thought you'd be working this morning."

"I have employees for a reason," she says as she walks into the room carrying three coffees. "I brought goodies."

"Bless you," I mutter, reaching for the paper bag she's carrying. "Fresh croissants make everything better."

"For you," she says to Cash, passing him a coffee. "There's a protection spell in there."

"Does it have eye of newt?" he asks, flashing a smile.

"Not this time," Millie replies with a wink, making Cash's smile slide from his face. "And I might have put a little spell on the pastries, as well. We can't be too careful. We don't know what we're dealing with here."

I'm already sitting on the couch, my legs crossed under me, happily eating my way through the bag's contents.

"I'm so damn hungry," I say with my mouth full.

"Probably all that walking you're doing in your sleep," Cash says calmly.

"What?" Millie's eyes fly to mine. "Where did you go?"

"I didn't physically go anywhere. I wasn't sleepwalking, I was dream-walking."

"Oh, I've *always* wanted to do that," Millie says with excitement. "I didn't know you could."

"I didn't either. And, trust me, it wasn't nearly as fun as it sounds."

"I'm going to let you two talk while I go get my things from Andy's house."

I frown up at him. "You're moving in?"

"I told you, I'm here for as long as you'll allow it. I can't protect you from my brother's home." He leans in and kisses my head. He hasn't kissed me on the lips yet, and it's killing me. "Since you have Millie with you, I'll run over there now. I'll be back shortly."

"I don't need to be babysat, you know."

"There's strength in numbers," he says, his handsome face completely sober. "And until all of this is resolved, I'd rather you weren't alone."

He hurries out of the apartment, and Millie watches him walk down the street through the window.

"He's hot."

"I know," I say and reach for another croissant. "I should probably have some protein with this."

"That one has turkey and cheese in it," she says, watching me carefully. "Where did you go in your dream, Bri?"

"I was walking in the Quarter." I take a deep breath. "Toward work. Everything was normal until it went dark. Suddenly, the two women were standing before me."

"The sun went down?"

I frown, thinking about it. "No. More like something covered the sun."

Millie leans forward. "A cloud?"

"A shadow." I blink rapidly. "A *shadow* covered the sun."

"Okay, keep going."

"I could hear the girls. They kept saying that I needed to find them. Help them. But when I tried to ask questions, no sound came out of my mouth."

"Fascinating," Millie says. "Did they say where they are?"

"No. They didn't give me any other information. It's so damn frustrating."

"I wonder what happened to them?" Millie asks.

"They were tortured."

It's her turn to blink rapidly in surprise. "Excuse me?"

"You heard me."

"How do you know?"

"Because I could see it." I swallow hard and tell her what I saw. "It was awful. I wish they were still just shadows."

"I'm so sorry you had to see that," Millie says softly.

My phone rings. "Holy shit."

"Who is it?"

"Daphne." I hold Millie's gaze as I answer the phone. "Hello?"

"Hi." My sister's voice is quiet. I've missed it so much. I feel tears spring to my eyes. "I know we have our issues right now, but I've been dreaming, Bri. I feel like you need me."

"I do." *And not just for this.* "How are you?"

"I'm fine, but those girls aren't."

"You've seen the girls?"

"And you," she confirms. "Last night, I saw you talking to them in my dream."

"I didn't see you."

"I kept trying to get your attention, but it was no use. It was damn frustrating."

"Come over. Millie's here, and we can talk about it all."

"I'm working today," Daphne says with a sigh. "But let's go out for dinner. We can talk then."

I agree, and we end the call.

"It's not just you," Millie says.

"No, she says she had the same experience I did last night." I shake my head in disbelief.

"That means I'm next." Her smile brightens. "And I'll be ready."

"She'll be here," Millie assures me. We're at our favorite restaurant in the Quarter, Café Amelie.

"She's ten minutes late. Daphne is never late."

"She'll be here," she says again as she reads the menu.

"Maybe she changed her mind. I could tell she wasn't thrilled to be talking with me."

"One of the things we need to clear up tonight is this stupid fight y'all have been having for more than a *year*. It's ridiculous."

"I—"

"Sorry I'm late." Daphne hurries to the table and sits in the empty seat next to Millie. She looks *amazing*. Her red, curly hair is weaved into a simple braid, and her golden eyes look tired.

She's a sight for sore eyes.

"I've missed you—" I begin, but she holds up a hand, stopping me.

"I'm not here to talk about the issues we have," she says. "Let's get that straight right now."

She moves to shove a piece of paper into her bag, but I stop her.

"Where did you get that?"

She frowns and glances down at it. "A lady on the street gave it to me. Asked me if I'd seen her before."

"Let me see."

She passes it to me, and I stare down at a photo of Tammy. Her last name is Holmes. She was only twenty-four, visiting New Orleans from Wisconsin.

"This is one of the girls."

"I didn't recognize her," Daphne says, looking at it again. "Of course, I wouldn't. She didn't look like this last night."

I swallow hard. "No. She didn't."

"Two things need to happen tonight," Millie announces, taking control of the conversation. "One, you *will* figure out a way to get past this stupid fight."

Daphne starts to argue, but Millie shakes her head, shutting our baby sister up.

"And two, we need to figure out what's happening to these poor girls and decide what we're going to do about it. Where's Cash?"

"Who's Cash?" Daphne asks.

"He's a new person in my life," I reply. "I told him I

was going out for dinner with my sisters, and that I'd see him later."

"So, you've already moved on from Jackson, then?" Daphne asks, glaring at me from across the table.

I reach over and hold Daphne's hand in mine. "I need you to talk to me, Daph. We can't get past things if you keep shutting me out. I did *not* do anything inappropriate with Jackson."

Her eyes fill with tears at the mention of his name. Jackson was Daphne's high school sweetheart. They broke up when he went into the military, and when he returned, he asked me to meet up with him for lunch.

Daphne walked in on us and immediately assumed the worst.

"I saw it with my own eyes."

"You saw us having *lunch*."

"He had his damn hand on you!"

"You acted like a child," I counter, completely frustrated with my little sister. "You threw water in his face and stormed out as if you'd found us in bed together."

"Oh, trust me, I'm relieved that I was spared that much."

"Ew." I lean back and stare at her in horror. "Jack has always been like a freaking *brother* to me, Daph. I would *never* do that, no matter what. He's for you, and I'm not the least bit attracted to him. How could you even think that? We've gone more than a *year* without speaking, all because you assumed I jumped into bed with your boyfriend?"

"He's *not* my boyfriend," she whispers and dabs at the tears on her cheeks. "And even if it was just a simple lunch, it doesn't matter. He came back, and rather than reach out to me, he reached out to *you*. Do you know how horrible that feels?"

"It wasn't the right time," Millie says calmly.

"For the love of the stars, Mill, just let me be a woman for five minutes, okay? It hurt me, and I'm entitled to feel that way."

"Sure, you are," I agree, surprising her. "You feel betrayed. But you let it fester all this time and wouldn't even let me explain. You *assumed* I was bouncing all over the man you love, and that's pretty harsh, Daph."

"I'm not sorry," she says softly. "You should have called me right after he asked you to meet."

"He's my friend."

"He's my *everything*."

I sit back and study her. If the tables were reversed, and we were talking about Cash, how would I feel?

Hurt, certainly.

But I like to think I'd give them both the chance to explain.

"So, even though we didn't do anything inappropriate, you're going to continue taking your anger out on me? That's not fair."

Daphne pouts for a moment, then sighs and wipes the last of her tears away. Daphne's always been the most dramatic of us, but she's never behaved like this before.

"You're right," she says at last. "It's not doing any good. And, frankly, being angry all the time is exhausting."

"I can only imagine. I don't want you to be mad at me."

"Let's table this for now," Daphne says.

"Wait. Does that mean you're speaking to her again?" Millie asks.

"Yes, I'm speaking to her." Daphne rolls her eyes. "Now, let's get to the real reason we're all here." She points to the paper still sitting on the table.

"I'll fill you in on what's been happening so far." I go back to almost a week ago when I first met Cash, and tell her everything, from the moment I first saw him, to seeing the new shadow, and then the apparitions last night.

Has it really been less than a day?

It feels like months.

"And you haven't experienced anything?" Daphne asks Millie.

"No, not yet. But my shields are strong, and I'm super careful to center and ground myself. I have to."

"I know," Daph says and pats our sister's shoulder. The waitress arrives to tell us about the specials and take our orders. Once she's gone, Daphne clears her throat.

"So, there's something else I should tell you guys." She glances at each of us, then ducks her head as if she's embarrassed or ashamed. "I went to see Mama."

"What?" Millie and I bark in unison.

"Why would you do that?" Millie asks.

"She called me," Daphne says.

"I didn't know she had electricity, much less a phone," I say.

"She went to Horace's house to call," Daphne says. "She sounded real bad and made me feel guilty, so I agreed to go."

"No," Millie says, shaking her head emphatically.

"I wasn't there long," Daphne says. "The inside of the house is awful."

"What did she want?"

"I don't know." Daphne shrugs. "Once I got there, she said she didn't remember calling me. It was weird. She was mean. And you know as soon as I stepped inside..."

She shivers, and Millie and I both put our hands on her, giving her our strength—both literally and figuratively.

"We'll go to the café after this," Millie says. "I have potions for you to take."

"I appreciate it," Daphne says, adding a nod. "We can't ever go back there, guys. Not ever."

"And we never will," I assure. "Now, what do we do about this?"

I point to Tammy's missing person poster.

"We talk to Cash," Millie says.

"Why?" Daphne asks.

"Because he's with the FBI," I reply. "And he's a

profiler."

"Wow. You snagged yourself a cool boyfriend, Bri," Daphne says.

"He's hot, too," Millie informs her. "And has a good heart."

"You looked?" Daph asks.

"Of course, I did. She's my sister."

"YOU'VE MULTIPLIED," Cash says with a smile when we walk into my apartment an hour later.

"I'm the youngest sister," Daphne says, sending Cash a little wave. "Daphne."

"Cash. Pleasure to meet you."

Cash turns to me and pulls me in for a lazy hug. "How are you, darlin'?"

"Not too bad, actually. Sorry we're later than I thought. We had to swing by the café to get some protection potion for Daphne."

He narrows his eyes as he glances at my sister. "What's going on?"

"It's quite a story," I say and gesture for him to have a seat with me on the couch. Millie sits in one chair across from us, and Daphne takes the other.

"Whoa," Daphne says in surprise.

"What?"

"Someone had sex in this chair."

Cash's head whips around to me, and I hold up my

hands in surrender. "It wasn't me. I haven't had sex in... well, we don't need to go there."

"Not you," Daphne confirms and then laughs. "I don't know where you got this chair, but I like it. Whoever owned it was happy and quite playful."

"Well, that's fun," Millie says, grinning. "You should re-christen it later. After we leave."

"Thanks for the pointer," I say with a laugh.

"It's not a bad idea," Cash says, making me grin.

"Focus, please."

"I had the same dream that Brielle did last night," Daphne begins. "And when I was on my way to dinner, a woman stopped me on the street and gave me this."

She pulls the missing person flyer from her bag and passes it to Cash. He reads it, then looks at me with sad, green eyes.

"I remember her from the tour," he says.

"So do I. It's the same girl I see."

"Can you see them now?" Millie asks.

"They're outside," I inform them. "They don't follow me inside. Probably the wards or the crystal grid."

"Are they on the sidewalk?" Daphne asks.

I stand and peek outside. Sure enough, the two women are on the sidewalk, staring up at my apartment.

Talk about creepy.

"Yep."

"So, we know now that Tammy at least has been

reported as missing," Cash says thoughtfully as I sit with him.

"She's dead," I say.

"We know that," Cash replies. "But the authorities don't. I'd like to consult with my brother on this."

"He's a cop here in New Orleans," I inform my sisters, then turn to Cash. "But what kind of cop?"

"He works in robbery," he admits.

"We have another contact," Millie says. "We just need to ask Miss Sophia. There are a couple of detectives who have worked with psychics in the past."

"Mallory Boudreaux's grandmother," I reply, remembering. "I need to go into Mal's shop this week anyway. I'll ask for her contacts then."

"If she doesn't know, Miss Sophia will," Millie says.

"I don't want to sit on this," Cash says. "There could be more girls missing."

"Cash, I don't have any proof, and I don't have any information aside from knowing she's dead. And, trust me, most people—especially cops—don't believe in psychics. They'll blow me off for sure. At least until I have more information or some proof."

"This is damn frustrating," he mumbles, rubbing his fingers over his lips. "In the meantime, I'm going to run searches in my database to see if other women with similar descriptions are missing."

"They do look alike. And they look like someone else," Daphne says thoughtfully.

"Who?" Millie asks.

"Brielle."

All eyes turn to me in surprise at Daphne's statement.

"You're right," Millie says. "At least, Tammy does. We don't know anything about the other girl."

"She resembles her, too. At least from what I could tell in my dream." Daphne shakes her head.

I stand to pace. I think better when I'm moving.

"Is that why they're coming to me? Because they look like me? Maybe they're trying to warn me or something."

"It's possible," Millie says as I walk past the window and glance outside.

"Shit," I mutter. "Guys? There are now three girls."

CHAPTER SIX

"One side of me says, I'd like to talk to her, date her. The other side of me says, I wonder what her head would look like on a stick?"

-Ed Kemper, AKA the Co-ed Killer

I t's possible that he went overboard this past week. But after such a dry spell, and once he got the taste of the woman he took from Brielle's tour, he just couldn't help himself.

"Hello, dear," he says to one of the five girls he currently has tied up in his room of fun. She's the most recent, and she hasn't stopped crying since she woke up this morning.

Of course, he doesn't find the show of emotion attractive in the least.

It's a weakness.

And that means this one won't last long once he starts playing with her.

Pity.

"Now, Brielle, there's no need to cry."

"I'm not B-B-Brielle," she whimpers. "I'm Ally."

He backhands her across the face, making her lip immediately bleed.

"You'll learn."

But she doesn't stop crying. No, she just sobs louder.

If he were a less patient man, he'd just slit her throat right now.

But that won't do. No, he went through too much trouble bringing her here, taking her out of a bar with plenty of people around to see.

She was too perfect to pass up.

He'll just have to listen to her cry.

Unless...

"Here, Brielle, this will help." He grabs a bloody rag from his workbench and stuffs it into her mouth to muffle her cries. "There, now. Much better."

He ignores the other three tied to their beds, some slipping in and out of consciousness, and one weeping quietly into her bare mattress, and then turns to the girl strapped to his chair. He clicks his tongue when he sees the blood running down her thigh from where the leather has bitten into her innocent flesh.

"Oh, this won't do. You've been trying to get away, haven't you?"

Her eyes are glassy as she shakes her head, denying her own struggles.

"I'm the only one allowed to make you bleed, Brielle. I told you that before."

He reaches for the woman's hair and surprises her when he pours warm water over it, then begins to wash it with shampoo that smells like apples.

"It has to be clean," he says, his voice soothing and even. "Nice and clean."

Once the soap is rinsed, he painstakingly braids the long, dark hair, securing it with a black hair tie.

Then, once it's just the way he likes it, he reaches for the scissors and cuts off the braid at the nape of her neck.

"I'm keeping this," he says, his face stretching in a sinister smile. "It's my little trophy. You don't mind, do you?"

She shakes her head, making him chuckle.

"Of course, you don't. You're such a good girl, Brielle. Always so sweet and nice."

He returns to his workbench and hangs the braid above the window, joining the other twenty-nine plaits.

"Thirty," he mumbles. "The same as your age!"

He turns to her triumphantly, ignoring the cries and whimpers coming from the others, completely focused on the woman in his chair.

"Oh, that calls for something special. Something very special, indeed."

He flips on the switch of the car battery charger

next to the chair, parts her legs, and reaches for the cord.

"You're going to love this."

CHAPTER SEVEN

Cash

"There have to be more missing persons reports," I mutter as I power up my laptop. Brielle and her sisters sit nearby, talking about the new girl that's joined the other two apparitions.

My brother pointed out to me this morning that this could all be a scam. And I can't exactly say his hypothesis is wrong. Brielle could be making up everything she supposedly *sees*, all for the sake of being dramatic.

Or, she could just be plain crazy.

And, frankly, I don't know her well enough to say for certain that he's not right.

But it feels like she's telling me the truth. And my intuition is rarely wrong.

I've seen the scared look in her eyes when she sees something new. That fear isn't a lie.

So, until I can say for certain that they're all whacko, I'm in this for the long haul.

"It's cool that you have access to the Fed's files," Millie says and smiles.

"I'm hoping it helps us figure out at least a pattern," I reply, entering stats into the search engine.

Dark hair.

Blue eyes.

Average height.

New Orleans.

And then hit *go*.

I glance up to find Brielle's bright blue eyes focused on me. She's quiet, but her face is tight with worry. All of this is taking a toll on her.

How do I know that?

How is it that I just met her a few days ago, and yet I feel as if I've known her for ages?

"How are you, darlin'?"

She shrugs a shoulder. "I'm okay."

"Holy shit," Millie mutters, pulling me back to the task at hand.

"What?" Daphne asks, hurrying over. Brielle doesn't join us.

She knows.

"Dozens," I mutter, paging through the names, the photos. "I only put in a five-year time span."

"Extend it," Brielle says. "Go back ten."

I do as she asks and feel my stomach drop. "There are more, but not many. It seems the number is far less until six years ago. At least girls missing from New Orleans. I'm going to look through each one to get more information. We'll look for girls taken in the French Quarter to start, and then we'll expand from there."

"With that list, it'll take you all night," Daphne says.

"You guys can go home," Brielle says quietly. "Get some rest. Maybe we'll have more information in the morning."

"This is going to take time," I agree and nod. "Brielle's right. Get some rest, ladies."

"I'm exhausted," Millie admits. "And I need to look in on the café before I head to bed. But I'm a phone call away."

"Same," Daphne says. "I don't live as close as Millie, but I can be here quickly."

Both sisters flank Brielle, all of them wrapping each other in hugs. They quietly whisper something in unison, like a prayer, and then once they've said their goodbyes, it's just Brielle and me.

"How many do you think?" she asks.

"I haven't dug around—"

"Ballpark."

"A couple dozen, at least. Some of these cases will have likely been solved. But once I narrow it all down and weed through it all, there will still be a couple dozen unsolved, I'm sure."

She blows out a breath and scratches her nose. "What do you need from me?"

"Coffee. This is going to take a couple of hours at least. You should get some sleep."

"I'm afraid to sleep," she admits softly. "And that pisses me right off, Cash. I told you, sleep has always been my safe place."

"And it will be again," I assure her. "As soon as we figure this all out."

"I hope it's sooner rather than later."

She pads into the kitchen, and I watch as she brews me a cup of coffee, adding just the right amount of sugar and cream.

I've never told her how I take my coffee.

When she delivers it to me, I set my computer aside and pull her onto my lap, cuddling her close.

"How did you know how I take my coffee?"

She opens her mouth, then closes it again and gives me a shy smile. "I don't know. I just knew."

"It'll be handy having you around." I smack a kiss on her cheek and then set her next to me on the couch.

"For my coffee-making skills?"

"Among other things," I say absently while I sip my coffee and gaze at the computer screen.

"You've never kissed me."

I glance over at her. "I kissed you just a moment ago."

"On the cheek."

Ah, here we are.

"Does it bother you that I haven't kissed your sweet lips yet?"

She shrugs that shoulder again and blows out a breath. "Maybe."

"Once I start kissing you, I won't want to stop there. You're a game-changer, Brielle, and we're a little busy right now. I don't want to fuck it up. Do I want to put my hands on you? My lips? Hell, yes. Who could resist you?"

She blushes and opens her mouth, but I press my finger against her lips, shushing her.

"I want many things with you, and we'll get there. But in the meantime, I need to figure out how to get these damn dead people to stop tormenting you so I can have you all to myself. Is that what you wanted to know?"

She puckers those lips still pressed to my finger and kisses the tip of it lightly, then smiles.

"Yeah. That's what I wanted to know."

My computer beeps, drawing my attention.

"Okay, I've sorted out the unsolved cases, including the cold ones."

"Cold cases?"

"Don't you watch TV?"

"Not much."

I smile and answer her question. "Cold cases are those that are old and never solved, ruled to be unsolvable."

"Gotcha. That makes sense."

She leans against me, pressed to me from shoulder to knee.

Once I've weeded through the remaining results, I'm left with forty-two.

"Forty-two?" she asks, reading the tally at the top of the screen.

"Yeah, that's what we're left with. That doesn't mean he's killed all of these girls, though. They're just the ones that fit the general description. Some of the bodies were found, but the cases were never solved."

She swallows hard, then points to a photo in the middle. "She's the first one I saw."

I jot down the name and keep paging through, but it's not until we get to the more recent listings that Brielle points again. "There's Tammy."

"Do you see the most recent girl?"

She frowns, examining each of the women again, and then she points to the last girl on the list. "This one. That's her."

"You're sure?"

She nods and bites her lip. "Yeah. They don't look much like those photos now given what was done to them, but that's them."

"What do they look like, Brielle?"

"You don't want to know."

"I've worked on some horrendous cases. There's not much that can surprise me."

"It's not just that they've been beaten. One definitely was because her whole face is swollen and bruised. But it's more. They've been...tortured. Tormented." She stands to pace again. She seems to think better when she's moving. "One of the girls, the one who was beaten, was also eviscerated. Slit from throat to pubic bone. Her torso looked empty of organs."

"Christ."

"Yeah, I don't see them as they were when they were alive and happy. I see the horror. Every detail."

"I'm so damn sorry, Brielle."

"Me, too. It was way better when they were just shadows and they'd tell me what happened to them. I didn't have to *see* it." She plucks at her lip, thinking. "One of the other girls had a slit throat. And the third one was burned."

I swallow hard, hating that she's had to see all of that.

"So, here's what we know," I begin, all business-like, my voice full of authority. "He's consistent. He likes one type of girl and doesn't deviate from that type. Dark hair, blue eyes, average height. Maybe he has a mommy complex, and he's killing his mother over and over again. Or, he's a jilted lover. There's something about these women that makes him comfortable and turns him on."

"Turns him on?" she asks incredulously.

"Oh, for sure. He most likely gets an enormous amount of sexual gratification from killing these women. From the actual *act* of torturing and killing them. He's definitely a sexual sadist."

"Sick son of a bitch."

"Absolutely. He probably has a mental illness of some kind. He's likely a psychopath, at the very least a sociopath, and absolutely a narcissist. He doesn't see what he does as wrong. He's proud of it, but he understands right from wrong, and laws, and he's very good at covering his tracks so he doesn't get caught."

"He's a serial killer," she says, surprise lighting up her face.

"Of course, he is. This isn't new for him. He's been killing for many years, most likely longer than the six we know about. These are just the people with a missing person report. He probably started at a young age, brutalizing animals, then progressed to experimenting with the homeless and other people that he thought wouldn't be missed. He may not have killed right away, but it likely didn't take him long to progress to that."

"How do you live with all of that in your head?" she asks.

"I could ask you the same thing."

She shakes her head, glances outside, and then sits next to me again, leaning her head on my shoulder. "They're still out there."

"I suspect they're not going anywhere for a while."

She nods. "Sleep with me tonight. I don't want to be alone. Please don't leave me alone."

"I'm right here. I'll stay with you."

"Thank you."

"No dreams last night." She smiles up at me as we walk through the French Quarter. She's leading me to her friend's store, where she claims the owner will be able to direct us to the correct police officer to talk to.

I'd rather just call my brother and ask for a contact.

But I'm not the one seeing dead people. So, for now, I'll do things her way.

"I'm glad." I squeeze her fingers. "You hardly moved."

She was pressed to me all night, and I wanted to make love to her more than I've ever wanted anything in my life.

But it's not the time for that yet.

We'll get there.

"It's just around the corner." Brielle guides me down the sidewalk, and we stop in front of a store called Bayou Botanicals. "I absolutely *love* Mallory's shop. It smells good and feels amazing. Let's go."

I open the door and follow Brielle into a lovely store full of oils and soaps and other things I can't identify.

"Brielle." A redhead smiles and hurries over to hug Brielle. "It's so good to see you." I assume this is Mallory, and her face changes when she touches Brielle. Tightens. "Oh, friend."

"I'm okay," Brielle assures her. "I want to introduce you to Cash."

"Hi, I'm Mallory Boudreaux," the woman says, shaking my hand. Her eyes narrow on mine, and just

like when I first met Millie, I assume I'm being scruti-
nized in ways I can't begin to understand.

"Do you need more frankincense?" Mallory asks
Brielle.

"Yes, actually. And we came for another reason, as
well."

"I know," Mallory says with a small, sad smile. She
turns to me. "I'm psychic."

"It seems everyone I meet lately is."

"Fascinating," Mallory says. "And probably discon-
certing."

"Very."

Mallory reaches for a bottle and sets it on the
counter. "You need Miss Sophia."

"Well, I was hoping *you* would know who your
grandmother used to work with at the police
department."

"I was too young and way too angry," Mallory says.
"I hated that she worked with them. So, I don't have
any names for you, but Miss Sophia might. She's here."

"*Here*-here?" Brielle asks in surprise.

"She brought me some tea this morning. I thought it
was a casual visit, but I suspect she knew you'd be in
today." Mal winks and disappears into a room marked
Employees Only, then returns with an older woman. The
woman is small, but her face is free of wrinkles. She has
shiny, blond hair, and when she sees Brielle, her eyes fill
with tears.

"Oh, my sweet girl."

"I'm okay," Brielle insists as she's pulled in for a firm hug. "A little unsettled, but I'm fine."

Sophia cups Brielle's face in her hands and stares into her eyes, keeping perfectly silent for a long moment.

"There," Sophia says, "that should help for a while."

"Thank you. Miss Sophia, I'd like to introduce you to—"

"Cassien Winslow," the older woman says and crosses to me, her shrewd, blue eyes fixed on mine. "We've been waiting for you, haven't we?"

"You have?"

She steps closer. "You don't know?"

"I have no idea what you're talking about."

She takes my hand and closes her eyes. Suddenly, electricity shoots through my arm and down my spine. A quick movie of still images flashes through my mind. Brielle and I together, naked. Tears. Fear. Fire. Joy.

Holy shit.

"What was that?" I ask.

"A taste of what's to come," she says and leans in close to whisper words meant for only my ears. "You need to be clear of mind and strong of will for what's coming for you, Cassien Winslow."

"What's coming?"

"I can't tell you that. I know you're confused, but you were made for this. Literally. You're one of the six."

I frown, but she doesn't continue. She turns to Brielle. "What were your questions, dear?"

"We need to go to the police," Brielle says. "Cash is with the FBI, but we need local law enforcement, and I don't know who to go see that might actually believe what I have to say and not just blow me off as a loon."

"The police that worked with Mal's grandmother are all retired," Sophia says.

"Oh, that's too bad," Brielle replies.

"I'm sure we can ask to speak with whoever is in charge of missing persons and go from there," I suggest, then find all three pairs of eyes on me. "What? We have information about missing women. That's how it works."

"Not for us," Sophia shoots back. "Not everyone trusts the words of a witch, Mr. Winslow."

"Is that what you are, Miss Sophia?"

She flicks one finger, and suddenly, I'm in the center of a strong wind, swirling around me. Just me. I go from hot to cold and back again until she flicks that finger once more and everything calms.

"Point taken." I smile at the older woman. "I meant no offense."

"Oh, none taken, dear. That was just a friendly demonstration."

Mal and Brielle laugh.

"I suggest you talk to a man named Asher," Sophia says.

"Have you worked with him before?" I ask.

"No, I've never met him." Sophia's calm eyes meet

mine. "I know things. Asher will help you. And, Cassien, you need to call your mother."

My eyes widen. "What do you know of my mother?"

"Just call her," Sophia says, then she turns to Brielle and kisses her cheek. "They'll keep talking. Listen carefully."

"Yes, ma'am."

"SHE DIDN'T ANSWER?" Brielle asks when I shove my cell into my pocket and hold the door of the NOPD headquarters open for her.

"No. I'll try again when we're finished here."

Now I'm worried. My mom has battled health issues for the last several years. I text Andy and ask him if he's heard from her today. Hopefully, he has.

"How can I help you?" a uniformed woman asks from behind bulletproof plexiglass. Her name tag reads *Lewis*.

"Is there an Asher that works here?" Brielle asks. "I'm sorry, I don't know his last name."

"Lieutenant Smith," Lewis says and nods. "I'll call back and see if he's in his office."

"Appreciate it," I say with a smile, and we wait while Lewis makes the call, talks into the phone, and then nods.

"He'll be up to get you in just a moment."

"Thank you," Brielle says, her smile forced as she

walks to the other side of the small waiting area with me.

"What's wrong?"

"Lots of shadows here," she says with a sigh. "But they're all shadows. Not apparitions. She has one looking over her shoulder."

"Wow."

Brielle nods. "This building is two hundred years old, so it's not unusual for there to be lots of activity. It's just not part of my usual routine, and—"

"You don't like surprises," I finish for her.

"Hello."

We turn at the man's voice. He's tall with jet-black hair and tanned skin.

"Asher?"

His eyes narrow on Brielle. "Yes, I'm Lieutenant Asher Smith."

"Lieutenant, I'm Cash Winslow. I'm with the FBI, but I'm here in an unofficial capacity. Also, I'm armed."

I show Asher my badge and my gun, much to Brielle's surprise.

"I didn't know you carried a *gun*," she hisses.

"Thanks for the heads-up," Asher says. "I'll ask you to leave your weapon with Lewis. We'll give you a receipt for it and give it back when you leave."

"Understood," I reply. It's standard procedure.

Once my gun is locked away and I have my receipt, Asher leads us back through the bullpen to his office. He shuts the door and gestures for us to sit.

"How can I help you?"

Brielle licks her lips and glances over at me. "I don't know where to start."

"Start at the beginning," I urge her. "That's always the best route."

She nods, looks at Asher, and starts her story.

"I see the dead."

Asher's brows climb into his hairline, but he listens quietly as she walks him through all of the events, step by step, from the night I met her until now.

Before he can reply once she's finished, there's a knock on his door, and a woman pokes her head in. "The body found this morning has been identified. Tammy Holmes."

"Thanks."

The female officer nods and shuts the door behind her.

"I think we're going to have to come back to this," Asher says. "I have a full plate right now—"

"I know what happened to her," Brielle says, her voice taking on a hint of desperation now.

Asher's eyes narrow on Brielle. "Go on."

"She was beaten severely. Her face was almost no longer recognizable." Brielle shakes her head, then describes the way the victim was cut open, and all of the other atrocities done to her.

When she finishes, Asher sits back in his chair, staring across his desk silently.

"You don't believe me," Brielle whispers.

"This is New Orleans," Asher says. "I've seen a lot of things in this town. But we haven't released any of that information to the press."

"I don't need you to," Brielle says, raising her chin.

"Okay, then tell me how you can help. Were you there? Did you *see* him do those things to her?"

"No, I see things after the fact. As I said, I see dead people. The girls came to me, but they haven't told me how to find them yet, just that I *have* to find them. I already told you that."

"Listen. I have a dozen missing girls, all with the same MO. We finally found one in the bayou this morning, which just confirms my worst suspicions. I need more to go on. The fact that they're simply *dead* doesn't help me. I need to know where, how, when."

"I know," Brielle whispers.

"What do you do for the FBI?" Asher asks me.

"I'm a profiler."

He looks between Brielle and me, then slides his card over to me. "Keep me posted. In an official capacity, I'm not ashamed to admit that I could use you on this case, Cash."

"I can ask to be assigned to it," I offer.

"Let me request it, officially," Asher says. "I'll put that through this morning."

"You're going to let us help?" Brielle asks.

"Him," Asher says, pointing to me. "Because he has a badge and the knowledge I need. But I want to know if and when you know more."

"Okay."

We stand to walk out of the office. Brielle walks out first, and Asher asks me to hang back.

"I also want you to keep an eye on *her*," he says quietly. "For protection, and to make sure she's not dicking with us."

"She's not," I assure him. "And I know you're bringing me on so you can keep an eye on us. This isn't my first rodeo."

"As long as we understand each other."

CHAPTER EIGHT

Brielle

"At least he didn't look at me like I'm crazy," I mutter when we walk out of the police station, Cash tucking his gun back into its holster under his pant leg. "Why didn't I know you've been carrying that?"

"You never asked me," he says with a crooked grin. He pulls his phone out of his pocket and frowns down at it.

"What's wrong?"

"Andy says he hasn't heard from our mom today. I'll try to call her again." He holds the phone to his ear, listening to it ring. "Mom! I've been trying to reach you all morning."

His shoulders sag in relief, and I slip my hand into his free one, giving it a supportive squeeze.

"Are you feeling okay?"

I tune out the conversation and glance behind me. There are only two girls following me now.

Tammy's gone.

Is it because they found her body and now she can be at peace?

Is *peace* what they each want?

I wish I could talk to them, understand what in the world is going on.

I wonder if the only way to figure this out is to allow myself to dream-walk again. To ask questions and be more present in the moment and less afraid.

To be fair, it was a surprise last time.

But if I'm more prepared, I might be able to make it work in my favor.

"I'll talk to you soon."

Cash hangs up and sighs in relief.

"How is she?"

"Tired," he says. "She says she's just tired, but I talked her into going to the doctor."

"I'm glad. I suppose we should stop in to see Millie at the café. And I should call Daphne."

"No."

I stop on the sidewalk and stare up at Cash. "What? Why?"

"No, we're going to take a few hours just for us."

I'll admit, I was embarrassed last night when I blurted out that he hadn't kissed me yet. I'd like to chalk it up to exhaustion and sexual frustration.

But it's probably more about me being socially awkward.

"Say something," he says.

"What do you want to do?"

"Anything, as long as it's with you, we're not talking about murder or death, and I can get to know you better."

"You want to go on a date? At eleven in the morning?"

"Dates happen at any time of day," he reminds me. "And, yes, that's what I want. Let's take a break. We've done everything we can for now. Until Asher or my boss calls to let me know I'm officially part of the investigation, there's nothing more for us to do."

He brushes his knuckles down my cheek.

"I'd like some time alone with you."

"Death follows me wherever I go," I warn him, but he just smiles.

"Yes, but we don't have to dwell on it, do we?" He kisses my nose and leads me back to my apartment and his car, which he parked at the curb yesterday. "I want to take you somewhere."

"Okay." I sit in the passenger seat. Once he's started the car, he pulls away and heads across town, away from the French Quarter.

"I asked my brother to tell me where his favorite restaurant is away from the Quarter," Cash informs me. "I think we need a little break from there. We'll have a nice lunch, then go from there."

"It's not part of my usual routine, but I admit that it sounds nice." I settle back against the leather of the seat and take a deep breath. It feels good to let someone else make plans. "I work tonight."

"No."

My head whips around so I can stare at him. "Excuse me?"

"Don't you think you should take some time off until we get a handle on this?"

"No, I don't." I shift in my seat to face him fully. "First of all, you don't get to tell me what I can and can't do, Cash. Second, I have to work. I have bills to pay. And trust me when I say it's not cheap to live in the Quarter."

"This sicko's taking girls, torturing and killing them, and they look exactly like *you*."

"I'm well aware."

Two of them are sitting in the back seat of his car, but there's no need to tell him that.

"Give me one week," Cash says as he guides the vehicle into a parking space and turns to me with beseeching, green eyes. "Please, just give me a week. I'll pay your rent this month. Hell, I'll pay for everything."

"That's not—"

"I'm scared," he admits and reaches for my hand. He kisses my knuckles and then looks back at me. "If he were to take you, I would never forgive myself."

"One week," I confirm. "I'll give you that. I'll make a call once we're inside."

"Just like that?"

"I don't know many men who would freely admit that they're afraid," I reply. "Most give an order, stomp their foot, and expect the little woman to fall in line."

"I'm not an asshole."

"No. You're not. So, yes, I'll agree to a week. You don't have to pay my rent, though. I'll be fine."

"Thank you," he whispers, then gets out of the car. He opens my door and leads me inside a new building that houses a Mexican restaurant. "New construction. Not remodeled, *brand new*. No ghosts here."

I smile, touched that he put some thought into choosing the place. Of course, there are ghosts every-where, no matter when the building was built.

But I won't tell him that and rain on his parade.

"I hope you like Mexican food."

"It's actually my favorite."

"I ATE MY WEIGHT IN CHIPS." I pat my belly as he drives back toward my apartment. We agreed to head over because his boss called while we were having fried ice cream. Cash is officially part of the investigation. "Why can't you stop eating them once you start? They're like crack."

"It's the fried ice cream that does me in," he confesses. He pulls up in front of my building and follows me upstairs.

"When do you have to go report in?"

"Tomorrow morning," he says with a smile. "I can get most of the information remotely. And I'm not leaving you today."

"I don't—"

"Need to be babysat," he finishes for me. "I know." He shuts the door behind us and advances on me, prowling.

The look in his amazing green eyes is hot as fuck.

"I'm not here to babysit you," he says as his hands slowly loop their way over my hips and around my back.

"No?"

"Nope." He kisses my forehead. "I have other things in mind that don't involve sitting."

"No sitting."

He smiles and kisses my cheek. His body is warm and firm, and his hands rub delicious circles over my back.

"Not unless we decide to rechristen that chair Daphne talked about," he says. His hands glide over my butt, and he suddenly lifts me effortlessly, supporting me with his palms under my ass, carrying me to the bedroom.

"Are you ever going to kiss me?"

"Eventually." The lips that I want so desperately on mine twitch into a sly smile. He lays me down in the middle of the bed and crawls over me, dragging his nose over my clothes, sending shivers down my spine and causing goosebumps to rise.

My back instinctively arches off the bed in invitation.

"God, you're amazing," he whispers against my neck. He places a wet kiss there, then drags his lips up to my ear. "Sexy as hell. Keeping my hands to myself for a whole week has been complete torture."

"But not keeping your lips to yourself?"

He smiles down at me. "Now I feel a lot of pressure to do this right. What if I'm really bad at it, and you're expecting fireworks?"

"You're not bad at it."

"You don't know." He kisses the apple of my cheek. "I could be a dud in the kiss department."

He kisses the corner of my mouth, teasing me relentlessly.

Finally, *finally*, he presses those hot lips to mine and sinks in.

This man doesn't merely kiss and call it a day.

No, he kisses like it's his damn job. Like kissing me is the only thing in the world he can think about.

As if he's wanted to kiss me for decades.

I sigh, push my fingers through the hair at the nape of his neck, and hold on as my body comes to life under him. His hand cups my breast over my shirt, his thumb brushing over my puckered nipple.

We're fully clothed, and I've never been so turned on in all my life.

"So sweet," he whispers before changing the angle of the kiss and diving in all over again. I'm drowning, and it's the most intoxicating thing I've ever experienced.

"Am I a dud?"

I lick my lips and narrow my eyes as if I'm thinking it over.

Honestly, I just can't make coherent thoughts form yet.

"Brielle."

"I like the way you say my name."

He quirks a brow. "How's that?"

"Like it feels good on your tongue."

"Your name isn't the only thing that feels good." He licks along my jawline. "You make me crazy, you know?"

"No, I didn't know."

"Well, you do now." His lips cover mine again, and his hand tugs my shirt out of my pants. He kisses and undresses me as if it's effortless.

As if he does it every day.

The air is cool against my naked skin.

"Goosebumps," he whispers before suckling my nipple, then blowing on it.

I had no idea it could get harder than it was.

But it can. It does.

And he's still dressed.

"If I'd known you were hiding all of this talent, I would have attacked you days ago."

He chuckles and lets me pull his shirt over his head so I can get my hands on his warm, smooth skin.

He's tanned.

Toned.

Has muscles for days.

And for now, he's all mine.

"You look like the cat who ate the canary," he says.

"Oh, I'm pleased for sure." And in just a mere ten seconds, I have him naked, his heavy cock resting on my belly as he kisses me silly.

I work him over, gently at first, and then with more aggression as he hardens more in my grasp.

"Condoms," he mutters.

"Drawer." I point to the table beside the bed and grin when he finds an unopened box.

A girl should always be prepared.

Even girls who never get laid.

You just never know.

I take the little packet from him, tear it open, and with my gaze glued to his, I roll it down his length, enjoying the way his jaw clenches from the pleasure.

"Keep touching me like that," he mutters, pinning both of my wrists over my head with one of his big hands, and positioning himself at my slick entrance, "and I'll blow this before we even get started."

"Oh, I'm having a good time so far."

"Just good?" He pushes inside of me and seats himself, pausing. "We can do much better than *good*, sweetheart."

Before I can retort, he covers my lips with his again and starts to move, rendering me completely thoughtless.

All I can do is feel.

Him. Us.

And how this seems familiar.

———

"PAST LIVES," Millie suggests the following morning. "That would explain it."

I just finished telling her about the day before. Sex for hours. Sighs and laughter.

More orgasms than should be allowed in any twenty-four-hour period.

And how it all felt like we'd done it before.

"I don't even know for sure if I believe in that."

"I do," Daphne says. "It's written somewhere, isn't it?"

I frown at my baby sister. "What, past lives? Like in a book? I mean, people have been telling fictional stories about it for ages."

"No." Daphne shakes her head impatiently. "It's on the edge of my memory, but I swear we've seen it somewhere before."

"The book," Millie says, snapping her fingers. "Remember that old book we found when we were kids?"

"Oh, yeah. Where is that?" I ask, shocked when Millie shrugs. "What do you mean you don't know?"

"Mama took it away from me when I was sixteen

and refused to give it back. It was just a few weeks before we all moved out of there."

"You never told us that," Daphne says.

"I was afraid you'd get mad at me for getting caught," Millie admits. "I don't have it, guys."

We look back and forth between us, dread settling in.

"We said we'd never go back there," I remind them.

"That was before," Daphne says. "We *need* that book. Grandma wrote it for us."

Our grandmother was a witch, and she wrote a book of spells and prophecies and random magical knowledge that she hid in the house. We found it when I was about fifteen, and we all pored through every page.

We didn't know Grandma practiced the craft.

No one ever told us.

Then again, our parents mostly ignored us.

"How are you able to make your potions?" I ask Millie.

"Lots of practice. I memorized most of them, and whenever I have a question, I just ask Miss Sophia and add it to my own grimoire."

"I can't believe you never told us." I rub my stomach. It's already full of butterflies—and not the exciting kind—at the idea of going back there.

That house almost killed us all once.

"We have to go together," Daphne says.

"Mom won't let us in," I remind them. "She's crazier

than ever, and mean on top of it. She certainly won't willfully give us that book."

"It's ours," Millie says. "I never should have given it to her."

"It's not like you had a choice back then," Daphne reminds her, patting her shoulder. "Sometimes, you got the worst of it."

Millie is the spitting image of our mother. Tall and blond and absolutely beautiful. Once upon a time, our mom was, too.

Not anymore.

"We don't necessarily need the book right this minute."

My sisters stare back at me.

"Past lives, apparitions, evil things happening," Daphne says, ticking off the items on her fingers. "Sure would be helpful to have a handbook right about now."

"Okay, I get it." I sigh deeply. "I don't like it, but I get it."

"When should we go?" Millie asks.

"Tomorrow." I square my shoulders as if I'm preparing for war.

Because I am.

"I want to go with Cash. There's strength in numbers, like he said."

"Are you sure you want to show Cash where we grew up?" Daphne covers my hand. "It's not pretty. No one would blame you if you wanted to keep him as far away from that as possible."

"He won't leave me because we grew up poor." I shrug. "I don't know how I know that, but I do. I'm not proud of where we grew up or how we did, but I'm proud of what we've accomplished since we got away from there. I think Cash would prefer to go with us than have us go alone."

"She's right," Millie says. "He should go."

"Tomorrow it is, then."

CHAPTER NINE

*"I was born with the devil in me. I could not help the fact that
I was a murderer, no more than the poet can help the
inspiration to sing."*
-H. H. Holmes

"You weren't there!" He slaps her across the face, disgusted when she cries out in pain. "You think that hurts? You wait. Just wait, you little piece of shit."

"Please," she cries, begging. She's beseeched him for days, pleaded with the monster to let her go. "I won't tell anyone, mister. Honest. I just want to go home."

"Shut up!" He hits her again. Rage is a beast roaring through him. It's Tuesday. Brielle *always* works on Tuesday. She has Monday off, and that's when he rests and plays with his toys.

On Tuesdays, he goes back to following her.

But she stood him up tonight.

She'll pay dearly for that.

"I was going to go easy on you," he mutters as he assembles his tools. "I was in such a good mood, Brielle. I was going to make it sweet."

The smell of urine and blood hangs in the air, still fresh from late last night when the electricity finally took the life of that last one. She moaned in pleasure for hours, screamed his name as she came.

She loved it, just like he promised her she would.

But it was eventually too much for her.

It always is.

"Let her go, you sick fuck!"

He spins and pins the girl he took two hours ago with a look that has made others piss themselves in the past.

But not this one.

No, she's feisty.

She shrugged off his medicine, and she's been fighting against her restraints the whole time.

He'll break her, just like the wild horse she is. He'll remind her of her place, and who's in charge.

And when the life finally leaves her filthy body, he'll celebrate.

"Now, Brielle, that's not polite."

"I'm Sarah Chandler, you sick son of a bitch. And I'm going to kill you."

This makes him smile. Oh, he loves a challenge.

Secretly, he sometimes enjoys it when they fight back just a little.

He can't let them know that, though. No, he has to maintain his standards.

She's going to be fun.

But first, he has other plans. He turns back to the whiny little bitch on his table and snarls.

"You made me mad tonight, Brielle. Do you know what happens when I get angry?"

"Please," she whines. "I swear, I didn't do nothin' to you, mister."

"You're not so innocent." He hits her again with the leather belt he keeps by the table, just for fun this time. Her flesh immediately welts and turns bright red. "Now that's a pretty sight."

There's crying and mewling behind him. Six women can make more noise than a barn full of pigs.

"No one can hear you." His calm is back as he turns to look at each of them. "You can scream and cry all you want, Brielle, but no one will ever hear you. You're never going to leave here."

He breathes deeply, satisfied that his little toy has soiled herself.

He reaches for the hacksaw.

"Here we go, Brielle. Now, be a good girl."

The work is messy. It's a good thing he bought the heavy rubber aprons years ago to keep his clothes clean.

And, of course, he covers his hands, hair, mouth, and

eyes so there's no chance he can contaminate his toys with DNA.

That wouldn't do.

The blood spatters and sprays as he cuts. Piercing screams rend the air. Thrashing ensues.

And then, her blue eyes focus on his as, little by little, the life slowly drains from her.

"Ah, that's a good girl."

He's hard. Killing always leaves his cock pulsing, but he never gives himself the pleasure of release.

Not for this one.

Or any of these.

But soon.

CHAPTER TEN

Brielle

"It's bad." Cash and I are sitting in the backseat of Daphne's car. He holds my hand tightly. "Like, whatever you consider to be bad, multiply it by about a thousand, and it's still not bad enough."

"I'm sure it's fine," he replies and kisses my hand.

"No, it's not fine," Millie says from the passenger seat. "B's not lying. In fact, it could be worse than what she's describing."

"It is," Daphne confirms, and my stomach clenches.

Maybe they were right. Perhaps bringing Cash to my mom's house was a bad idea.

Except, that place is a house of horrors for me, and Cash seems to ground me. Maybe he can steady all three of us. I know that's asking a lot, but when it comes to this, I'm asking.

And I'm not sorry.

Daphne turns off the freeway and points the car deep into the bayou.

"Did y'all grow up in this house?" Cash asks.

"Until Daphne was about fourteen," Millie says. "Then Brielle was old enough to move out, and she took us with her."

"Mama didn't try to stop her," Daphne adds.

"Bri saved our lives," Millie says quietly.

"That might be a bit of an exaggeration," I reply, but both of my sisters shake their heads emphatically.

"You know it's true."

"Are you saying you would have died from neglect?" Cash asks.

"Psychological and spiritual warfare," I say calmly.

"Jesus."

"Pretty sure Jesus and the rest of the deities out there helped keep us alive," Daphne says. "Pastor Cliff spoke with us. Prayed for us, often. I might have gone crazy without him."

"Witches who believe in Jesus?" Cash asks, a smile on his face.

"Don't overthink it. We're complicated women," Millie replies. "I forgot how damn creepy it is out here in the middle of nowhere."

"Live oaks are beautiful *and* creepy," Cash agrees, watching the bayou pass by. "And this looks like it belongs in a horror movie."

We all go silent as Daphne navigates onto another smaller road, and then it turns to dirt.

"You just went white as a ghost," Cash murmurs to me.

"I've never hated a place more." I take a deep breath. "You ladies know what to do."

We're reinforcing our shields, protecting our minds and our hearts from the horrors we're about to see. Millie casts a spell of protection around Cash, as well, and I'm grateful for not only that but also the protection potions she put in our coffees this morning.

We need all the help we can get.

The lane narrows even more, the path overgrown with low-hanging limbs and Spanish moss. It clearly isn't traveled often, if at all. With the exception of Daphne visiting the last time she came here.

"A part of the road washed out during a storm at some point, so it's going to be extra bumpy here in a minute. Hold on," Daphne says as she slows down, taking it easy over the ruts. She turns another tight corner, and there it is.

"Holy shit," Millie whispers when Daphne stops the car. We all sit in silence for a moment, staring at the house we grew up in.

It doesn't look habitable. Actually, it's *not* habitable, but Mama lives there anyway.

It was once a grand, three-story plantation home with a deep, wrap-around porch. Gas lanterns hung from the porch, along with a swing on either side of the red front door.

It's no longer grand.

The porch has separated completely from the main structure and caved in on itself in several places. The space around the front door looks to be intact, but I'll suggest we go up one at a time when we approach, just in case.

"Someone lives here?" Cash asks quietly. "Has it always looked like this?"

"No. Not when we were kids, at least. But this is what the bayou will do to a building if it's not maintained. It reclaims the land."

"Every single window is broken out," Millie says. "And in the stifling heat of summer. How does she not get heatstroke?"

"Who cares?" Daphne asks. "Let's get this over with."

"You three are with me, at all times," Cash says. "I'm armed."

"We can't fight what's in there with a gun," I inform him but squeeze his hand gratefully. "But, yes, we'll stick with you."

We climb out of the car and make our way gingerly up the dilapidated front steps.

I pound on the door.

There's no movement for a while. Just the sound of cicadas and frogs and whatever animal is rustling through the bushes.

I pound again.

"This was a bad idea," Millie says and turns to me. "What do you see?"

"The usual. More shadows than I can count, all staring at us. Walking the grounds, sitting where that old swing used to be over there."

"Just standing here gives me the heebie-jeebies," Daphne says. "I will *not* touch anything inside. I'm sorry, guys, but even the doorknobs—"

"Agreed," I interrupt and then pound on the door again.

"Go away!" Mama yells from inside.

"Well, we know she's alive," Cash mutters.

"Mama, it's us," I yell back. "We need to talk to you."

The door is yanked open, almost coming clean off the hinges.

"What the fuck do you want?"

I don't know who this woman is. The tall, beautiful person who raised us is gone. She's hunched over, her blond hair gray and stringy. Her teeth are missing. Her eyes are cloudy, the pupils dilated as if she sits in the dark all the time.

From the stench coming through the door, I'd wager that she hasn't seen a bar of soap in years.

"We need to ask you some questions," I reply. "Do you know who we are?"

"Don't matter who you are," she says. "Don't care."

"We're your daughters," Daphne reminds her. For a moment, it looks like her eyes might clear and that she'll remember, but then she just frowns.

"Don't got no chillins."

"Yes, you do," Millie says kindly. "We won't take up too much of your time. We just have some questions."

"Don't know nothin'," she mutters but moves back away from the door to let us in. All four of us cover our mouths and noses with our shirts, overwhelmed by the smell of filth and death.

"Mama, are there dead animals in here?" I ask.

"Hafta eat, don't I?"

We look at each other and follow after her as she shuffles through garbage and insects. Where the dining room used to be is a pile of debris from the old bedroom—*my* bedroom—above it. The ceiling collapsed at some point. My old twin bed, such as it is, lies on the top of the heap.

The mountains of garbage are horrifying as we move through the old living space toward the kitchen. But it's the stench that I'll never forget.

I'll have to burn these clothes later.

I'll never get the smell out of them.

"Where do you sleep?" Cash asks, and Mama rounds on him.

"Who the hell are you?"

"This is my good friend, Cash," I say. I bet most girls don't introduce the guy they're hot after to their mom that way.

Lucky me.

"I don't talk to no mens," Mom says.

"It's a good question," Millie says. "With the second floor collapsed, where *do* you sleep, Mama?"

"Oh, where'd my manners go?" I frown as I watch our mother smile and push back her hair as if she has unexpected company. "I meant to clean up 'fore'n you came by, but I must've got busy with the chillins."

"Your home looks fine," Daphne says as if she's talking to a stranger, and I immediately take her cue. My youngest sister has done her best not to touch anything, but I can see the strain on her face.

"I agree," I say. "You keep a lovely home."

"Well, thank you kindly," Mama says with a tooth-less, satisfied grin. "Hasn't been easy to keep up with them girls since I done killed their daddy."

She winks, to my horror, and gestures for us to follow her to the den off the kitchen.

I trade glances with the others and follow her, surprised at what we see.

Where the rest of the house is utterly condemnable, this room isn't so bad. She keeps the door closed from the rest of the house. She has a simple twin bed made neatly with old blankets that I recognize from my child-hood. There's an oil lamp and a rocking chair in the corner.

The chair that used to be under the stairs.

The one where a shadow still sits, rocking back and forth.

"That thing never stops movin'," Mom says and shrugs. "Probably uneven boards or somethin'."

"Or a ghost," Daphne whispers, catching Mama's attention.

"We don't talk like that in this house, young 'un," she says sternly. "There be no ghosts here, y'hear me?"

"Yes, ma'am," Daphne says quietly.

"These girls, always carry'n on about ghosts and goblins." She shakes her head as if it's all nonsense. "Now, what can I do for you?"

"Mama, do you remember a book that you took away from Millie when she was a teenager?"

Mom narrows her dull eyes as if she's thinking.

"Can't read," she says simply, surprising me.

I didn't know that.

"It was a book that *I* was reading, and you took it away from me," Millie adds. "I really need it back."

"I burn all the books here so I have heat," Mom replies with another shrug. "Probably burned that up, too."

"Do you mind if I look around for it?" Millie asks.

"You're plum stupid if you think you should wander around through this house. It's full of evil spirits," Mom says, shocking all of us.

One minute, we don't talk of ghosts.

The next, the place is full of evil spirits.

I mean...she's not wrong.

But her mental illness has clearly progressed so much that it's hard for her to make any sense.

"I'll be careful."

"Don't matter to me." Mom waves her off.

"Go with Cash," I say instantly. "None of us goes alone."

Cash squeezes my shoulder, then follows Millie out of the room.

"Y'all can sit," Mama offers, pointing to the bed as she sits in the rocking chair, right on the shadow. "We're not too fancy in this house."

"I'm fine," Daphne says immediately but smiles to soften the rejected offer. "How are you doing?"

"Same as always," Mama replies. "Ain't nothin' change 'round here."

Except the number of spirits. I don't know why, but they seem to have multiplied considerably. Doubled, maybe even tripled. Everywhere I look, another shadow lurks.

No wonder she's crazy.

I would be, too.

"You know, if you ever want to leave this place, there are people who can help you."

Mama narrows her eyes at me. "Tryin' to run me outta my own house?"

"No, ma'am," I say immediately. "It was just an idea."

"This place is nice enough. My girls never complain."

"Your daughters are all grown," Daphne reminds her. "We're your daughters, Mama. Remember? We all grew up and moved away."

She frowns as if she's confused. "But I talk to y'all every day. You visit me here all the time."

One of two things is happening here. Either Mom is

simply certifiably nuts, or the spirits here are taking our shapes to mess with her.

At this point, it could be either.

Or both.

"I haven't set foot in this house in more than a decade," I remind her.

"Who are you?"

"I'm Brielle."

"Brielle's dead. He killed her."

My skin prickles. My heart skips a beat.

"Who killed her?"

"Killed who?"

I sigh in frustration. She can't focus on a conversation long enough to make a logical statement.

"What do you do here all day with no electricity or running water?" Daphne asks.

"There's water out back," she says, pointing over her shoulder toward the swamp. "I wash my clothes in there."

She washes her clothes in swamp water.

It's a wonder she hasn't been eaten by 'gators or died from a bacterial infection.

"I just talk to my friends, an' I keep a pretty garden outside. Did you see it?"

"No, ma'am. There's a garden?" Daphne asks. Our mother did like to garden when we were kids. We spent a lot of time out there with her.

"I'll show you."

She pulls herself out of the chair, and we follow her

through the house to the back entrance, right next to the door that leads to the storage space under the stairs.

I spent the majority of my childhood under there.

I wait for Mom and Daphne to go outside before I open the little door really quick to poke my head in.

It hasn't changed since the last time I was in there with my sisters. It's as if Mama never went in there, but she must have at some point. She pulled the rocking chair out.

I close the door and join Daphne and Mama outside, just around the corner of the house.

Mom's smiling.

Daphne's face is white.

"Can you please tell Brielle what you told me?" Daphne asks her.

"Oh, is Brielle here?" Mama glances over at me and frowns. "I thought you were dead, Brielle. That's what he told me."

"Who told you that?"

"Don't remember." She rubs her nose with the back of her hand. "Anyway, he's buried right here."

"Who?"

"Your daddy." She rolls her eyes. "Never liked him. Mean son of a bitch."

"He was mean," I agree with a nod and stare at all the blooming roses. There must be twenty bushes, a riot of beautiful color. "You must spend a lot of time out here, taking care of your roses."

"Nah, he just keeps fertilizing them. Mean old man."

She shakes her head. "Told me I was crazy. Can you believe that?"

"No, ma'am," Daphne and I reply in unison.

"Kept callin' me that over and over again until I showed him just how crazy I could be. Buried him right here."

Daphne swallows hard, her hand hovering over a bloom.

I need to get her out of here.

"We found it," Millie says as she and Cash come around the side of the house. "We saw you out here."

"You have a beautiful garden," Cash says.

"Who are you?" Mama demands, her face immediately scrunching in rage. "I don't like the mens around here. Git outta here. Y'all leave, now."

"Gladly," Daphne says as we hurry around the house to the car. She starts it, and once we're all inside, she peels out of the driveway, watching Mama in the rearview. "Brielle."

I look back, shocked to find the shadows joining Mama, huddling around her. They're pouring out of the house, coming around the sides, and they cover her, wrapping their arms around her.

It's the creepiest fucking thing I've ever seen in my life.

"You can see that?" I ask Daphne.

"We all can," Millie says and sighs.

"I can't," Cash says.

"You're lucky." I rub my hands over my face. "But at least we have the book. Where was it?"

"Upstairs, in her old bedroom," Millie says.

"It's still intact?"

"If you can call it that," Cash replies. "We looked around the entire house, just to check everything out."

"I wrapped us both in my shields," Millie says. "And it's a damn good thing I did. Did you guys notice how out of control the activity is there?"

"It's like a hotspot for paranormal activity," I say, thinking it over. "I never considered that before, but that might be the case. Perhaps the house is built on a burial ground, or something so horrible happened there in the past that the ghosts are drawn to."

"And because we're sensitive, it fucked with us as kids," Daphne says, nodding. "It makes sense."

"Now that we're gone, along with our spells and potions of protection, there's nothing there to protect Mama from the activity," Millie says. "You guys, I know she was a bad mother and, honestly, she's a bad *human being*. But no one deserves that kind of torment."

IT DOESN'T SURPRISE me when the dreams come. After spending the morning doing my best to deflect the atrocities in my mother's house, I figured I'd have a difficult time in my dreams.

"Come on."

Now, there are four. When I went to sleep, there were still only two spirits following me, but now there are four.

"I want to help you. Tell me what to do."

"You have to follow us," one of the girls says, and relief immediately sets in. They can hear me. This one's new. She has a slit throat, but aside from that, she looks whole. "Come on."

The next thing I know, I'm standing in a room. It's good-sized, sectioned off into different areas. In one corner, there's what looks like a workbench with shelves above it, lined with tools.

A chair sits in another corner. It looks like an old-timey electric chair with leather straps on the arms and legs.

In the third corner is a door, presumably leading to the rest of the house.

And then there's the fourth corner, where there are currently four women tied to what looks like toddler beds. The tiny mattresses are bare. Some have blood and pee stains.

The smell in the room is as bad as my mother's house, but lingering with the stench of feces and urine is the metallic scent of blood.

So much blood.

And fear.

The girls can't see me. I try to talk to them, to get their attention, but they can't hear me. I need to ask them questions.

Where are they? How did they get here? Who brought them here?

Without those answers, this is pointless.

"Who are you?"

I'm surprised when another girl glances up and talks to me.

"I'm Brielle."

Her eyes widen, and her lip quivers. "He's going to kill us. He's going to kill all of us. And then he's going to kill you."

"Who is he?"

She shakes her head. "He's the devil."

CHAPTER ELEVEN

Cash

"I dreamed," she says as she walks into the kitchen from the bedroom. Her hair is a mess of dark waves around her beautiful face, her blue eyes look sleepy and tormented.

I've only known her a week, and yet I miss the happy look she had in her eyes before all of this started. She was quick to smile. To flirt.

Now, it seems she's wrapped in an invisible, heavy blanket.

I'm going to do my best to get her back to the happy woman I first met.

"Talk to me." I pull her onto my lap, and she reaches for my coffee, making me smile. I don't mind sharing it with her. Hell, I'll share my life with her if she'll have me.

That thought shocks the hell out of me.

My job is too intense to have a family. It's best to be

single, without ties to anyone.

But now that Brielle's in my life, I can't imagine it without her.

"More walking," she says with a sigh and leans her head on my shoulder. "But this time, I was in the room where he holds them."

"What?"

"He has four right now. One saw me, but I didn't get much information out of her."

"So, you don't know where he's holding them?"

"No. And it pisses me off, Cash."

"Well, it doesn't make me happy, either. I have to be in the office in about an hour."

"I'm coming with you." She kisses my cheek, then hops off my lap and sets to work making her own cup of coffee. "I need to talk to Asher."

"You don't want me to talk to him?"

"No. I have questions, and I need to prove to him that I'm not a whack job."

"I think if that was the case, he wouldn't have asked for my help," I remind her as I slide my hands over her hips and around her waist to hug her from behind. "You smell good."

"Neroli oil," she says, smiling up at me. "It's good for anxiety. And, I'll be honest, this whole thing has me more than a little anxious."

"You wouldn't be human if it didn't." I kiss her hair, then turn her in my arms so I can pull her in for a strong hug. "Maybe you need a break. I'll see if Andy and Felicia can join us for dinner."

"A distraction might be nice, especially after being in the bayou yesterday."

It was an experience I *never* want to repeat. I was honest when I told her that very little surprises me.

And yet, I was shocked as hell.

The living conditions were foul. The woman who birthed the three girls I've come to care about was... sick. That's the best word I can use for it. She is mentally ill for sure, and that's probably the root of the neglect of her children. But the fact that she admitted to killing her husband means that I'm under obligation to have her arrested.

Though it wouldn't matter.

She's already locked up, undergoing a far more brutal punishment than the government could ever throw at her.

"My sisters warned me not to take you there."

"Why?"

She leans back to quirk her brow. "Come on. You know you want to dump me after seeing where I came from."

"Dump you? No. I don't want to do that." I kiss her forehead and make slow circles on her back with my palm. "I have about a billion questions, but I don't want to lose you."

"I can probably answer your inquiries."

"I think the one person who could answer the bulk

of them the best is too mentally ill to do so. She belongs in an institution."

"I know." She rubs her face and then leans her forehead on my chest. "I know she does. But she'll never willingly leave that house. It has its claws in her."

"She admitted to killing your father."

"She did kill him." She looks up at me again. "And he continued tormenting my sisters and me for the better part of a decade afterwards. Speaking of him, I need to know what Daphne saw when she touched the roses yesterday. Whatever it was, it freaked her out."

"What made him stop tormenting you?"

"Millie met Miss Sophia, and she helped us get rid of him. He beat us repeatedly when he was alive, and then he taunted us from beyond the grave."

"A lovely man."

"He probably deserved much worse than what Mama gave him."

"Do you know how she killed him?"

"No, she never said. In fact, until yesterday, she never admitted to killing him—that I know of anyway."

"But you knew she did?"

"One day, he was there, being an asshole of epic proportions. Hours later, he was gone, she said he was never coming back, and we had a new shadow in the house. I was old enough to put two and two together."

"I see." I nod and back away from her. "I won't make any calls to have her picked up. But if I did, and they put her in an institution, it would be better than where she is now."

"Let's get through this, and then we can worry about my mother," she suggests. "One thing at a time."

"Deal."

⁂

"So, you're telling me he's currently holding four more victims," Asher says, observing Brielle carefully.

"Yes."

"Because you saw it in a dream."

She blows out a breath and starts to pace. "There are now four girls following me. They came to me in the dream and told me to follow them. Then, the next thing I knew, I was in a room with four *living* girls. It looked like a torture chamber."

"How so?" He starts taking notes. "Tell me what it looked like."

"It was a big room." She closes her eyes and begins to describe a workbench with tools, an electric chair, and the beds where the girls were tied up. "It's filthy. They soil themselves there, and there's so much blood by the workbench. Mostly dry, but there was some fresh blood, as well."

"Look on the walls," I instruct her as if I'm talking to a hypnosis patient. "Are there photos? Is anything written there?"

"Nothing's written," she says quietly. "But above the workbench, he has a bunch of things pinned in a line."

"What is it?"

She opens her eyes and looks right at me. "Hair. Braided hair."

"How many?" Asher asks.

"Thirty-two."

I take a deep breath. "He's killed thirty-two girls since he started this phase of his hunt. The braids are his trophies."

"I hope you're right. Because if I can get my hands on that hair, I can positively identify the victims and give the families some answers," Asher says, then turns back to Brielle. "I need you to do this again, but I need more information. I need you to walk through that door and tell me who he is. And, most importantly, *where* he is."

"I don't know how to do that," Brielle says in frustration. "I don't know how it's happening in the first place, Asher. This is not one of my gifts. I'm a medium, and I have some psychic abilities, but dream-walking isn't something I know anything about. I've never done it before."

"Hey," Asher says, holding up his hand, his voice softer. "Brielle, I get it. This is scary, and...well, just plain shitty. I hate that it's in your head. But I have faith that you can do this."

"Why do you suddenly believe me?"

"I didn't *dis*believe you before," he says. "But we

haven't told anyone that the bodies show evidence of electric shock torture. Or that their hair has been chopped."

She blinks, thinking it over.

"How many bodies have you found?"

"Six."

"Six out of thirty-two," I say calmly.

"You're the profiler," Asher says, turning to me. "Why aren't we finding all of them?"

"He doesn't want you to find the ones you have," I reply. "Where did you find them? The bayou?"

He narrows his eyes, and I keep talking.

"He's a sick fuck, but he's highly intelligent. He's dumping the bodies in the bayou because he knows they'll likely get eaten by critters and there won't be anything left of them. So, if you found them, it's because they didn't have time to get eaten."

"The most recent was found by a swamp tour group. They saw her floating in the water and fished her out."

"That's horrible," Brielle says softly. "I'm going to let you two do your jobs. I'm headed over to Millie's for the day. She and Daphne are already there poring through the book we fetched from Mama's yesterday. Maybe there are instructions in there for dream-walking."

"I'll take you."

She shakes her head no. "It's not far. I'll text you when I get there."

She kisses me, and then she's gone.

"Watching someone you love go through something

this horrible is its own kind of torture," Asher says, watching me.

"I didn't think I was made for it. Love." I sit down again and sigh. "But she's it for me. And I've only known her for a week. It's fucking crazy."

"Not too crazy," he says, flashing a smile. "I didn't know my wife much longer than that when I knew she was it for me. And she was held and almost killed by a serial killer."

"Jesus. I'm sorry."

"It was a few years ago, and she's doing great now. But I know what it's like to be afraid for the woman you love. We're going to catch this bastard if it's the last thing I do. Now, the profile."

"He's intelligent," I continue. "Most of the bodies are long gone. Sadly, you'll never recover them. He isn't the type to bury them in the backyard or anything like that. But the braids are interesting. It tells me that it's likely the hair that draws him to his prey. The color, the length. What a killer chooses as his trophies is quite telling."

"Long, dark hair. Why that?"

"It's usually one of two things. Either he's killing his mother over and over again, or he's a jilted lover, and he's killing the woman who scorned him."

"That seems a bit dramatic." Asher rubs his fingers over his mouth in agitation. "They all look like Brielle."

"I know."

"That has to be the connection between her and the

victims. Do the girls know, after they've died, that she's susceptible to being taken? Are they trying to warn all of the brunettes in town, but because Brielle has gifts, she's the only one who can see them?"

"All of those are great questions. But, honestly, I don't know. That could be the case, *or* it's Brielle that he's killing over and over again."

"Do you think it could be one of *her* jilted lovers?"

I didn't before. I hadn't considered it because what man likes to think about the dudes that have boned his girl before him?

But it does make sense.

"It's the only thing I can think of," I reply. "And, yes, I'll be asking her for a list of her former boyfriends tonight."

"No man likes to ask his woman for a list of the guys that she used to have sex with. I don't envy you."

"Yeah, it fucking sucks. But so does thirty-two dead girls, with at least four more being held. My ego can take it."

"I like you, Cash."

"ARE you asking me for a list of the men I've slept with?" Brielle asks. We're standing in Witches Brew with Daphne and Millie sitting nearby, all of them gawking at me.

"Hear me out."

"I mean, most men just ask for a number," Millie says to Daphne. "Like, *'how many have you slept with?'* They never ask for a list of names."

"He's taking their hair as a trophy," I say, my eyes still on Brielle's. "They look like *you*. The spirits are coming to you as a warning. Or a plea for help."

"So, you think the killer is an ex-boyfriend?" Daphne asks. "Talk about a bitter dude."

"There are two," Brielle says simply, surprising me. "Devon Price and Simon Harp."

"Ew, you did it with Simon?" Millie asks, scrunching up her nose. Brielle rolls her eyes.

"Neither of them was jilted. Devon was a guy I dated briefly in college, but he moved on to my roommate, so that breakup was pretty self-explanatory."

"And the other?"

"He used to own the ghost tour company," she says. "I found out *after* the fact that he was married."

"I'll have Asher run a check on them," I mumble as I shoot the man a text, seething inside at the idea of Brielle being with men who clearly didn't care about or respect her.

"Anything else you want to know?" she asks tightly. "Favorite positions? Number of times, that sort of thing?"

"Now you're pissing me off."

"We're even then," she says. "I get that you're being a cop right now, but you're my...well, my something, and I don't feel comfortable with this conversation."

"Aww, isn't that sweet?" Daphne asks. "She called him her *something*."

"Super sweet," Millie says, resting her chin on her hand.

"We're right here," I remind them both. "This isn't a show for your entertainment."

"You should have asked us to leave then," Daphne says with a shrug, not apologetic in the least.

"I need to find him," I say and reach for Brielle, pulling her to me. "I need to find this asshole so we can move on with our lives. I don't care who these idiots are. They were stupid enough to let you go. They're meaningless."

"Unless they're killing girls," Brielle says with a nod. "Okay. I'm hungry."

"Let's go eat, then."

"I'M gonna go stay with your mom, Cash," Felicia says as we finish up some pecan pie for dessert. Brielle and I met up with Andy and his wife for a casual dinner, and it was the perfect thing to take our minds off everything going on.

"Really?" I frown. "Did she ask you to do that?"

"No, but when I spoke to her this morning, she said she was tired."

"That's what she told me the other day, as well," I say, nodding.

"I know it's almost impossible for Andy or you to go see her right now, so I'm gonna go check it all out. See how she is and find out if she needs anything. I wish we could talk her into moving here with us."

"She's a stubborn woman," Andy says, patting his wife's back. "And we appreciate you going to check on her."

"He's right, on both accounts," I say with a nod. "I've been worried about her. I'm glad you're going to check on her. Please let us know if she—or you—needs anything."

"Oh, I will."

I pay the tab, and the four of us walk through the Quarter together. The restaurant isn't far from Brielle's apartment, so Andy parked there, and we walked over together.

"This building," Brielle says, pointing across the street, "used to be called Lafitte's Blacksmith Shop. The original owner, all the way back in 1722, was Jean Lafitte. He was a privateer and used the shop to cover up his illegal activities. It's now a bar. Patrons have said, after a drink or two, they see Lafitte in all of his pirate garb."

"I mean, I see a lot of things after a drink or two," Felicia says with a chuckle.

"Well, there's that," Brielle says, smiling. "But I can say, and I'd never put this in my tour, that Lafitte is certainly still in residence. In fact, he's currently standing in the window, watching as we walk past."

"And now it's creepy," Felicia says with a shudder. "You really *should* put this stuff in your tour."

"No way," Brielle says. "I would get too many questions, and the hecklers would be off the charts."

"You're probably right," Andy says. "So, you can take us on private tours and tell us all the extra-scary stuff."

"Trust me when I say, the French Quarter has seen atrocities you don't want in your head," Brielle says, carefully selecting her words. "Sometimes, the scary stuff, as you put it, is entertaining. But there are times that it's more than that. And if you feed into it, it'll follow you home."

"I don't want to know more," Felicia says, shaking her head. "No more for me."

Once at Brielle's apartment, we say our goodbyes, and I lead Brielle upstairs. While she puts her leftovers in the fridge, I walk into the bathroom and draw her a hot bath.

"I didn't know you were a bath man."

I turn to find her leaning her shoulder on the door-frame, watching me with a smile.

"This is for you. I think you could use a little pampering tonight."

"Are you just trying to suck up after asking me about my former lovers?"

"No." I kiss her nose. "I'm just taking care of you because I'm worried about you."

"Well, that's lovely." She kisses the palm of my hand,

then presses it against her cheek, leaning into my touch. "Thank you."

"You're welcome."

She crosses to the medicine cabinet and pulls out a bottle of bath salts.

"Here, you can use these."

"Do they have a special spell on them for protection?"

Her lips quirk into a smile. "No, they have lavender in them, which is good for relaxation."

"Just lavender?"

"I know, it's boring. But if you really want something magical—"

"No, this is fine." I pour the salts into the bath and gesture for her to climb in.

"You know, I was thinking about the killer this evening, and—"

"No. We're not talking about it tonight. We're going to rest and let our minds reset. There's nothing we can do tonight anyway."

She sighs as she strips out of her clothes, not self-conscious in the least to be naked in front of me, and steps into the steaming water.

"You know what, I can live with that."

"Me, too."

CHAPTER TWELVE

"I don't feel guilty for anything."

~Ted Bundy

W hat a pity.

He stares at the lifeless body on the small bed in disappointment.

He'd had plans for this one. So many wonderful ways he was going to play with her. He wanted to make it last with her, let her go for *hours* before he finally killed her.

She was special.

Of all his toys, she was the one who cried the least. She didn't really make any noise at all, and he was excited to see what it would take to hear that voice.

But instead, she found a way to hang herself with the ropes he used to tie her hands.

She didn't try to get away, which was interesting. She didn't untie the others.

No, instead, she used the rope to simply hang herself.

And if he were honest, that made him like her even more.

Though it was a pity that he couldn't play with her more.

"Ah, Brielle. Look what you did," he says as he untangles her from the rope. Her blue eyes are bulging, her face an interesting shade of purple.

But her hair is still long and soft.

So he lays her on the table and washes her hair, braids it, and cuts it for his collection. Even though he wasn't the one to finally end her life, he was ultimately the cause of her death, so he deserves the satisfaction of seeing her hair in his collection.

Brielle would want that for him.

He smiles in satisfaction as the hair joins the others, and then he carries the lifeless body outside and throws her over the railing to the swamp below.

She'll sink within minutes.

Either that or a 'gator will come for her.

He should really be considered a conservationist, given how much food he provides for the critters of the bayou.

With that thought in his head, he grins and walks

back inside. He really prefers to have more than three girls at a time, but since that one killed herself, he's down to just three.

That won't do.

"I'll have to go hunting this evening," he says with a sigh and sets his hands on his hips. "If I'm careful, I could take two. That's tricky, but I've done it before."

Neither of the remaining girls is crying. The one he's had the longest is sleeping. He checked her vitals earlier and verified she's still alive, just tired.

That's understandable.

He made one of the other girls rape her with a broomstick for about an hour this morning, and that'll tucker a girl out.

He turns to one of the other remaining girls and smiles.

"Hello, Brielle."

"Sarah," she responds coldly. "I'm Sarah."

He doesn't reply. Not at first. The anger is swift and hot, but he doesn't want to hit her. At least, not yet. The fire burns so fiercely in this one. He wants to draw it out a while. He needs to see how long it'll take before he finally breaks her mind, *then* he'll mutilate her body.

He's looking forward to it.

So, he simply leans in until his face is just inches from hers. He can smell the stink of her. If he put her outside, the bugs and rats would have a field day.

"You should thank me," he whispers. "I could make it so much worse for you than this."

She doesn't reply, just turns her head away in disgust.

He leaves her be and walks back to the sleeping girl. He pushes his fingers through her hair, enjoying the way the strands feel against his skin.

He's already getting hard.

"Brielle, wake up. We're going to have some fun."

CHAPTER THIRTEEN

Brielle

"*Come on!*"

It's happening again. Six girls gesture for me to follow them, and then suddenly, I'm back in the horrible torture room. It's daytime. Light filters through a dirty window, catching on the dust floating in the air.

There are still three girls, including the one who saw me last time, but the other two are different.

The ones who were here before are dead.

They helped to lead me here.

Knowing that he's already killed them makes my stomach sink. He's killing these girls so quickly that it seems he will make his way through many more before we find him.

Light shines under the door that leads to the rest of the house. I can hear he's listening to music.

Hello *by Adele blares through the room, barely muffled.*

I used to love that song.

Not anymore.

I need to get through that door so I can see who he is and where I am. I need to go back with information so we can catch him before he kills these poor girls.

I start to walk toward the door, but a voice stops me.

"It's you again."

I turn to find the girl from before staring at me. The same one from last time.

"You can see me?"

She nods and swallows hard.

"I never let him see that he scares me. My brothers always taught me to stand my ground, to never let them see you sweat." She sniffs. "I'm never going to see them again, am I?"

I don't know.

I hope she does.

"Sure, you will," I say and try to smile at her. It's only been a day since I last saw her, but I can see the fight leaving her. The fear, the torture, the torment are taking their toll. "You have to stay strong. You have *to keep fighting back."*

"It makes him mad. I talk back to him. I bit him when he tried to touch me."

"Good for you."

She turns, showing me her bare back where whip marks weep with blood. "I was punished."

"Please tell me your name. Tell me what he looks like."

"He calls us all Brielle.*"*

My heart stops.

"What did you say?"

"Brielle," she says again. "Like you."

Before I can ask more, someone tugs on my arm, and I turn

to see one of the spirits beside me, her eyes wide. "You have to wake up. Right now. Wake up, Brielle."

The phone rings beside Cash. He grunts sleepily as he reaches over and answers his cell.

"This is Winslow." He listens, and sleep leaves his face entirely as he looks over at me. "We'll be right there."

"What's happening?"

"The bastard tried to take someone tonight, but he fucked up. She got away."

"Oh my gods." I jump from the bed, and we hastily dress, then hurry from my apartment to Cash's car. There's no traffic at this time of night, and we arrive at the police station moments later.

"Cash and Brielle for Lieuten—"

"He's expecting you," the receptionist says immediately. She doesn't even ask Cash for his weapon as she buzzes us through, and we hurry through the bullpen to Asher's office.

Before he opens the door, Cash turns to me. "Let me do the questioning."

"I will."

He opens the door, but when we step inside, the office is empty.

"Over here," Asher says from behind us, gesturing for us to follow him. "She's in a more comfortable office. She's scared shitless."

"Catch us up," Cash says as we follow Asher down a long hall.

"She came in, crying and asking for help. She was out with friends and said a guy dragged her out of a bar on Bourbon. You can ask her some questions, as well. I don't know much more than that, she's only been here about fifteen minutes."

Cash nods, and we follow Asher into a small lounge. There are several comfortable chairs, one sofa, and a kitchenette that boasts coffee and little else.

It's definitely more comfortable for a scared girl than Asher's official office.

"Hi, my name is Cash." He approaches the girl with authority but does so gently. He squats in front of her, not too close, and doesn't try to touch her. The girl cries softly. "What's your name?"

"Shelly," she whispers. "Shelly Diaz."

"You're a brave woman, Shelly," Cash says, surprising her. "I'm proud of you. I'm sure you've already told Lieutenant Smith what happened tonight, but I'd like for you to tell me, as well. Take a deep breath and think it through. We need you to be as descriptive as possible so we can find this person."

"This all feels really extreme," Shelly says with a frown. "I mean, I thought I'd give a statement, but I don't know much. Drunk dudes must assault girls on Bourbon every single night."

"I'm sure they do," Cash says, nodding at the girl as he shifts the chair next to hers to face her, then sits in it. "But there's someone out there kidnapping and killing women."

Her eyes round, her hands clench, and all of the blood drains from her face.

"Holy shit."

"You might be the one person who can help us figure out who this bastard is, Shelly. So, we really need you to be as descriptive as possible."

"Holy shit," she says again and takes a deep breath, letting it out slowly. "Well, I didn't get a good look at him. The place was dark, and I was standing at the bar, waiting for a drink. Some guy came up to me and asked if I was having a good time. Told me I was pretty. It happens all the time, and that's not my ego talking, it's just the truth. Like I said, guys hit on girls in bars every night."

"I understand," Cash says. "Keep going."

"So, I didn't reply to him, just nodded. I didn't even look at him because I wasn't interested in being friendly with some strange dude. I have a boyfriend back home."

"Are you on vacation?"

"Yeah." Her lip quivers. "I'm here with some friends from Dallas. We drove over because I'd never been here before, and we wanted to have some fun."

"Go on," Cash urges.

"I didn't say anything, I just nodded. Then, this guy kind of pulls on my elbow, I guess to get my attention, I don't know. So I said, '*Look, mister, I don't want to talk to you.*' Sometimes, you just have to be blunt to make them go away, especially if they've been drinking. And, well, you know how it goes."

"Sure," Cash says.

"The next thing I know, he's tugging me through the bar to the exit. He's got a vise-grip on my arm, and he's just yanking me." Her lip quivers again. She lifts the sleeve of her top, revealing bruises just above her elbow. "I was yelling, but it was *so loud* in there. And crowded. There were people all around, but he told them we were just having a fight, and that he was taking me out where we could talk rationally."

"What a jerk," Asher mutters, catching Shelly's attention.

"He was more than a jerk," she says. "I've taken self-defense classes, and I knew that the worst thing I could do was let him get me alone or leave that bar."

"Good girl," Cash says. "You're absolutely right."

"I didn't think he was trying to *take* me, I thought he was trying to rape me. I've been raped before, at a party in college, and let me tell you, he didn't scare me so much as he pissed me right off. No man is ever going to do that to me again. Ever. So I fought back. But he was really strong. Like, way stronger than he looked."

"What did he look like?" Cash asks.

"He's not really that tall," she says, thinking it over. "Not much taller than me, I'd say. He has gray in his hair, and he's a white guy."

"A middle-aged white guy," Asher says. "Can you narrow it down a bit? Did he have any scars or tattoos?"

"Not that I saw," she says, plucking at her bottom lip as she seems to think it over. "I don't really know what his face looks like because I was trying to get away from him. I didn't stop to memorize it."

"You'd be surprised what you might have noticed," Cash says. "Did he have a big nose?"

"I don't think so."

"Wrinkles? Was he overweight?"

"He was average." She shrugs. "And I didn't see any wrinkles. He smelled, though."

"Like what?"

"Like a cat box." She wrinkles her nose in disgust. "Like a dirty cat box."

"How did you get away?" I ask, speaking for the first time. Her eyes find mine as if she didn't realize I was there until now.

"I kneed him in the balls and planted my elbow in his jaw, then ran inside. He'd shifted to turn the corner, and I saw the window of opportunity and took it."

"Wow, that's awesome."

She smiles at me. "You look just like my older sister, Lisa."

"What did he do when you got away?"

"He called after me, but I was already hurrying back into the bar. I went right to the bouncer and told him what'd happened. He stayed with me while I found my friends, and then they all convinced me to come see you."

"You did the absolute right thing," Asher says. "Everything you did tonight saved your life. You should be damn proud of yourself."

"I'm scared shitless," she says. "Do you really think he would have killed me?"

"Yes," Asher says simply. "I know your friends are waiting for you, but do you want a police escort back to your hotel?"

"No, we're driving right back to Dallas after this. I don't want to stay in New Orleans. It's safer at home."

"Just let us know if you change your mind," Cash says kindly. "And if you think of anything else, something he said or even the color of his eyes, call us right away."

"I have a question," I say, surprising them all. "Did he introduce himself when he approached you? Did he say, '*Hi, my name's Dave*,' or anything like that?"

"No." She sighs, frowning. "But he did call *me* a strange name. I never told him my name, and he kept calling me something. So, at first, I thought he had me confused with another person."

"What did he call you?"

"Brianne or something—"

"Brielle?" I offer, and her eyes light right up, confirming my worst nightmare.

"Yeah, that's it. It's different. Pretty. But not my name."

"Okay, thank you," Asher says and leads Shelly out of the room.

Cash and I stare at each other, not saying a word until Shelly is gone, and Asher returns.

"He's after *you*," Cash says.

"I just remembered that the other night when I dream-walked, the girl he's holding told me the same thing. She said he calls them all Brielle. I completely forgot."

"Now we need to interview *you*," Asher says, dropping into the sofa across from me. "Who the fuck is this guy?"

"I have no idea."

"He knows you," Asher counters. "And he's killing you, every fucking day."

I swallow hard as bile rises into the back of my throat.

"That's enough." Cash's voice is hard as he turns to me. "I checked out both of your ex-boyfriends. The guy from college lives in Arizona with his wife and two kids. The guy who used to own the tour group moved to Miami and got married last month."

"Good for them."

"So it's not a past lover," Asher says with a sigh. "A friend? A brother, cousin, childhood friend?"

"I don't have any brothers." My mind is whirling with possibilities. Who the hell could be doing this? "My father's dead. I don't have many male friends. Or friends in general, actually. They usually think I'm too creepy."

"Why?"

My smile is thin. "There's a shadow sitting right next to you. It has one ankle crossed over the other knee, and his arm is resting on the back of the couch as if you two are on a date."

Asher jumps up and rushes over to the kitchenette.

"There's a shadow standing to your left, right in front of the coffeepot. It's been moving back and forth from that spot to the sink and back again since we came into the room. It's as if he's making coffee over and over again. Which he very well might be doing. He could be stuck in a ten-second loop, repeating it over and over again for all of eternity like an echo. I don't know about you, but that sounds like its own kind of hell to me."

"Jesus Christ," Asher mutters, rubbing the back of his neck as if all of the hairs there are standing on end.

"I could keep going. I told you, I see dead people. It's who I am. So, if I'm going to be close to someone, they have to not only accept that fact, but they also can't be faint of heart.

"When I was younger, I tried to hide it from friends at school or boys I liked. I mean, who wants a creepy Debbie Downer around all the time, right? I know I don't. But, sooner or later, we'd be somewhere, and it would come out."

"Keep going," Cash says. When Asher frowns at him, he says, "This could lead to a light bulb moment."

Asher nods. "True. Keep going."

"Well, like one time in high school, I went to the movies with this guy I liked. Jeff Anderson. He was nice, kind of geeky. Anyway, he asked me out, and I said yes. We get to the theater, and it's an old one. There were so many shadows wandering around, it scared the hell out of me, and it takes a lot to do that.

"But I was young, and I *really* liked Jeff, so I just took a deep breath and sucked it up. We got our popcorn and Cokes, and when we walked into the auditorium, Jeff led me to seats in the middle of the place. But there were shadows already sitting there."

"What did you do?" Asher asks.

"I said, *'let's sit somewhere else.'* At first, Jeff was fine with it, but everywhere he went, there was a shadow sitting in the seat. Maybe it was the same one dicking with me. I don't know. That's happened before.

"So, finally, I said, *'this place is too haunted for me.'* He laughed, but when he looked at my face and saw that I wasn't kidding, he said some hurtful things, and we left. He refused to take me home. Said he didn't want a devil worshiper in his car. I had to walk home."

"All the way to that house in the bayou?" Cash asks.

"Yeah. It was horrible. The bayou is horribly haunted. I got home well after midnight, and my sisters were worried sick."

"What about your mom?" Asher asks.

"She slapped me across the face when I walked through the door."

"She's a lovely woman," Cash assures Asher. "So far, what I've learned from this is: I need to kick Jeff Anderson's ass, and your mom is a grade-A bitch."

"I won't disagree." I shrug a shoulder. "I know it's not Jeff doing this. The people who leave my life because of my abilities do so because it scares them. I don't have to be a shrink to know that. It's never made someone so angry that they wanted to kill me or anyone who looks like me. That would make them—"

"Psychotic," Cash finishes for me. "And, yes, it could happen. But I'm inclined to agree that it's unlikely. I'm also sorry that you had to deal with so many jerks."

"Everyone does."

"Are there any more shadows lurking around here?" Asher asks.

"Dozens," I confirm. "But those are the only two in this room. There's one that stands behind the receptionist. It looks over her shoulder as if its checking her work."

"My office?" Asher asks.

"None in there."

There *is* one in there, but there's no need to scare him.

"Well, thank Christ for that. And I'm at a loss for what to do now. The bastard failed tonight."

"That's going to make him angry," Cash says. "He'll strike again. If he hasn't already. And it'll escalate. He'll increase the speed in which he kills them."

"He's going pretty fast already," I say. "When I was there tonight, two of the girls were gone, and he had two more in their place."

"Wait, you were there tonight?" Cash asks.

"Yes. One of the dead girls alerted me to wake up."

"Were you able to ask questions? Walk through the house?" Asher asks.

"I was interrupted before I could walk through the door, but I was able to talk to the other girl again. The one who told me the killer calls them all by my name."

"What else did she say?"

"That she fights back, and she doesn't let him see that she's afraid of him. She has older brothers. That's really it."

"You have to do it again," Asher says. "Right now."

"I'm not able to *make* myself do it," I remind him. "I don't know what triggers it, aside from the girls being desperate for me to find their bodies. But Millie has been asking around and poring through the book. I'll go to her in a few hours and see if she's made any headway."

"I want to catch this son of a bitch before he kills anyone else," Asher says. "He's going down."

CHAPTER FOURTEEN

Brielle

"I'm dead on my feet."

"That's not funny," Millie says, frowning at me from behind the counter. We're at Witches Brew, and she's filling an order while I read through our grandmother's book.

Meme didn't have the best penmanship.

Some of it is hard to read. Either that or it's in another language, which is entirely possible.

"I want to add the love potion," Millie's male customer says, winking at her. "Let's roll the dice and see if it works."

"All I ask is that you take it outside before you drink it," my sister says, laughing. "If I had a dollar for every man who's fallen in love with me after drinking this, I'd be at least fifty dollars richer."

"I might fall in love with you without the potion," Flirty Customer says with another wink.

"Sorry, you're not my type," Millie says and flashes a sassy grin as she builds his vanilla chai latte and adds the love potion.

"What, you don't like devastatingly handsome, rich men?"

"I don't like *married* men," she replies smoothly, stirring his drink.

"How did you—?"

"I don't call it Witches Brew for nothing." She winks, and when she moves her hand away from the drink, it continues to stir without her, making the customer swallow hard. "I suggest, if you drink that, you do it while looking at your wife so you fall in love with *her* since you promised to do so until death do you part."

She passes him his change, offers him a friendly wave, and once he's through the door, she blows a loud raspberry through her lips.

"Dudes like that are disgusting," she says as she leans over the counter toward me. "Have you found anything good?"

"Not yet. Most of it is gibberish to me."

"That's because you don't speak witch." She frowns when her eyes drop to my neck. "Where's your pendant?"

"Oh." I reach for it, but it's not there. "I must not have put it back on after my shower. I'll text Cash and ask him to bring it with him when he comes this way for lunch."

I pull my phone out of my bag and shoot off the message, then frown down at the book.

"What if this doesn't work, Mill?"

"There isn't another option," she says and waves at another customer who just walked through the door. "Go ahead and sit anywhere. I'll be right over to take your order."

"I love your café."

Her grin is wide and proud. "Me, too. How does it feel in here today?"

I let myself look around the space. "No shadows."

"I smudged last night, and it should hold for a while. Are the girls still around?"

"There are six, but they stay outside. I don't know why they can't come in."

"Let's be frank here, I'm glad they stay on the sidewalks. It would just be awful if you had to stare at mangled bodies all day."

"You have a good point."

"Miss? We're ready to order."

Millie hurries over to the couple at the table in the corner, and I stare down at a yellowed page of the book.

The thing is huge. I've always seen big, magical tomes full of spells and recipes for potions in movies like *Practical Magic* or even *Hocus Pocus*, which always makes me laugh because my sisters and I look just like the Sanderson sisters—if we were evil witches, of course.

But I never expected these books to really exist.

Not until we found this one in the house under floor-boards in the little storage room where we hid.

"It has to be a hundred and three degrees outside," Millie says as she hurries behind the counter to fix the customers' drinks.

"Feels like it," I agree.

"How can people drink hot coffee on a day like this?" She shakes her head and starts up the steamer. "It perplexes me."

"I'm sorry I'm late," Daphne says as she rushes inside, carrying a large tote bag full of notes and books. "I've been at the library doing a little research."

"Wait, *you* went to the library?" I stare at her in shock. "Daph, that place must wreak havoc on you."

"Not fun," she agrees. "I can't tell you how many people have sex in libraries. It's disgusting. Not to mention, there were some books that people used to try and figure out how to kill someone and get away with it."

"Our killer?"

"Not that I could tell. No, mostly, they were people trying to off their spouses. It's just sad. Anyway, my shields are up, and I'm careful. Millie and I didn't find much in Grandma's book about dream-walking. Yet, anyway. There are some passages written in Cajun and a couple of others in what looked to be Latin that we couldn't decipher, and Millie's going to ask Miss Sophia what they say. In the meantime, I did some digging on dream-walking."

"Is there an instruction manual?"

"I wish." She digs around in her bag and slaps some books and loose papers on the counter. "Hey, Mill? Can I please get an iced chai? I'll love you forever."

"You'll love me forever anyway. But, yes. Do you want anything, Bri?"

"I'll have the same as Daphne, thanks."

"I'm adding some—"

"Yes, yes. Of course, you are," Daphne says, waving our sister off. "Now, as I said, there is no manual on how to do it. Unfortunately, like most things that are part of our reality, it's not really something that's been studied, and therefore, we don't understand exactly how it works."

"We already know all of that."

"But there *are* some interesting meditations and incantations in here that might help." She thumbs through the book until she arrives at the page she wants. We both accept our drinks from Millie.

"I have a call out to Miss Sophia, but there was an emergency with a coven up in Shreveport, and I don't know how long she'll be gone," Millie says.

"She'll get back to us soon," I say and sip my drink, then frown. "What's in this?"

"Two potions this time. It makes it a little bitter, sorry."

"You take all the fun out of lattes," Daphne says but sips her own drink. "Okay, it says here that you need to breathe deeply as you lie in bed and close your eyes.

Think about the place you want to travel to or the person you want to talk to. Or both, I guess. Have an imaginary conversation or think about the landmarks along the way from where you are to your final destination."

"Basically, literally go there in your head," Millie says.

"Yes, exactly." Daphne takes another sip of her drink. "Do it over and over again until you fall asleep."

"That seems too simple."

Both sisters glance up at me.

"Right? I mean, if it were that simple, people would have arguments with other people in their sleep all the damn time."

"Not everyone is psychic," Daphne reminds me. "And, maybe they do, but they just don't remember it the next day."

"Or they just chalk it up to a weird dream," Millie adds. "Most civilians pass off dreams or mystical encounters as something explainable. A bump in the night? The house is settling. They think they hear a voice? Must be the neighbor's TV."

"I get it," I reply with a sigh. "Okay, so don't make it hard. Simple is good. I need to lie down and breathe and think about that horrible place."

"I hate this so much," Millie says, covering my hand with hers. "I hate that you're the target and that you have to see these unspeakable things. It's not okay. None of this is."

"We've dealt with *not okay* since birth, my sweet sister," I remind her.

"It's your turn for okay," Daphne says, sighing. "Yes, I know I've been a bitch in the past about the whole Jackson thing, but you don't deserve this, Bri. I don't understand it."

"I don't either. I just wish I could see who he is."

Daphne turns to Millie. "You're psychic. Can't you see?"

"She can't reach out, Daphne. You know—"

"I can't see him," Millie says quietly. "I've looked, but I can't see him."

"Wait. You *looked?*" I sit back and stare at my sister in horror. "Millie, if you'd seen him, if you'd crawled into his head—"

"I didn't," she interrupts. "And you're my sister, Brielle. Of course, I looked, the consequences be damned. You'd do the same for me."

"I wish I'd known the girl was at the police station," Daphne says. "I might have been able to touch her and see him that way."

"Damn, it didn't even cross my mind." I shake my head. *Why didn't I think of that?* "She's long gone back to Dallas now."

"The dream-walking is the best bet for now," Millie says on a sigh and watches as her customers finish their coffees and leave the café.

"Should we talk quieter? This will creep the hell out of your customers," Daphne says.

"They can't hear us," Millie says with a smile. "And don't ask me how. You don't want to know."

"Speaking of creepy," I mutter and take a sip of my chai.

———

"I DON'T LIKE IT," Cash says quietly. "The investigator in me understands that this has to happen, but the man in me wants to say, '*hell no*' and take you out of here altogether."

"I know." I cup his face and let the warmth of him seep into me. It makes me feel comforted. Treasured. Safe. "But we have to finish this."

"Let me take you somewhere when it's all over," he says and kisses my palm. "Anywhere. An island somewhere. Or we can get lost in Europe."

"Europe might kill me." I smile and lean in to kiss his cheek. "But the island sounds lovely."

"An island it is, then." He clears his throat. We're lying on the bed, and I've told him how I go about trying to dream-walk intentionally. Both of my sisters are in the living room, on hand in case I need them to pull me out.

I don't know how they'll know if I need them, but Millie assured me that she would know.

I have to trust her.

And I do. There is no one in the world that I trust

more than the three people in my apartment with me right now.

I swallow hard, close my eyes, and begin taking long, slow breaths.

In through the nose.

Out through the mouth.

I don't know the way to where I'm going, so I can't think about that, but I do know what it looks like when I get there, so I imagine those details. I picture the dirty room, the blood on the floor, the dingy window. My nose wrinkles as I think of the stench. The heaviness that hangs in the room from the death and despair.

I wonder how many girls there have been. I know we think there were a few dozen at least, but I have a feeling there have been many more than that. I don't have to be a profiler to know that this isn't something he just started doing over the past six years.

He likes it way too much for it to be that new.

And if he's middle-aged, like Shelly seemed to think, he's likely been at this for decades.

I think of the girls. The six who continue to follow me, and the three in the room the last time I was there in my dream-walk.

I imagine the one who can see me, who talks to me.

I hope with everything in me that she's still alive.

"You're back."

It worked. I'm here! I glance at the girl and feel immense relief that she's still alive.

"And you're still here."

"He was mad tonight," she says, and her eyes flick to her left. Two more girls have joined the ones already there, making it five young women being held now. There are only three toddler beds against the wall, so the new girls sit on the floor, awkwardly tied to the bedposts.

They're both crying and shaking. He's stripped them naked, but aside from that, it doesn't look as if he's hurt them.

Yet.

And they can't see me.

"What's your name?" I ask the girl.

"Sarah," she whispers. "Sarah Chandler. But he calls us all Brielle."

"I know. But I won't call you that. You're Sarah. I want you to remember that. Hold onto your name, do you hear me?"

She nods quickly. "I'm Sarah. I have three older brothers, and I am a veterinarian."

"Wow, that's amazing."

A ghost of a smile tickles her lips.

"I'm going to look around, Sarah. I need to gather more information for the police. I need to know how to find all of you, okay?"

She nods again, and I walk away, headed to the door.

It's locked.

Frustration is swift and all-encompassing, but I turn and try to find other clues.

Maybe there are papers on the workbench. I walk that way and look around, disappointed to find it recently cleaned.

There's not even any blood on it now. No papers on the shelves either.

I glance around the room. There are no photos on the walls. Only the braids hang on the walls, and the roman numeral IV written in blood beside one of the small beds. Four.

Did someone cut themselves and then count the days until they died?

The thought sends a shiver through me.

I hear footsteps.

The girls whimper as the steps grow louder, approaching the door.

I'm going to see him! I'm finally going to see his face, and then I can tell Asher and Cash what he looks like, and we can find out who he is. We can put him away. We can make all of this stop.

The doorknob rattles.

The girls cower.

Sarah stares at me in horror.

But he doesn't come inside. There's a long pause, and then the steps fade away again.

The girls sigh in relief.

"He does that all the time," Sarah says. "It's just another way to fuck with us. Scare us. He taunts us mercilessly. Constantly. That's the worst part of all. Death would be a welcome escape from this hell."

"No." I rush to her and reach out, but my hand moves right through her.

I can't touch her.

I can't help her.

I've never been so damn frustrated in all my life.

The sun glints off something under Sarah's bed.

"There's a knife right under you."

Her eyes grow wide, and she struggles to see over the side. "I can't reach it."

"I have to get that knife into your hands."

I try to pick it up, but I can't grasp it.

Damn it!

Sarah looks at the girl sitting on the floor. "Hey, do you see a knife under my bed?"

The girl is crying.

"Stop crying and listen to me." That gets her attention. "I need you to pass me that knife."

The girl sees the weapon and uses her toes to pick it up and drop it on Sarah's bed. Sarah palms it in her free hand.

"You keep that hidden, and you use *it," I say strongly. "You're going to live through this, Sarah."*

"I hope you're right."

I WAKE with a start and blink rapidly, both of my sisters and Cash hovering over me.

"Are you okay?" Millie asks. Her face is lined with concern.

"I still didn't see him," I say and sit up to brush my hair off my face. "He's playing with them. Taunting them. He has five girls now. And there was a knife that he must have dropped. Sarah has it now, so if he tries to hurt her, she'll hurt him back."

"Sarah?" Cash asks.

"The one that can see me. Her name is Sarah. Sarah Chandler. She's been there a while, Cash. With the rate he's been killing these girls, the clock is ticking for her. And she knows it. But she's smart, and she's strong."

"She needs to be," Daphne says, her face pale.

"What's wrong?"

"She held your hand," Millie says quietly.

"You could see?" I ask.

Daphne nods and swallows hard. "It's something out of a horror movie."

"It's worse than that because it's real," I reply and reach out to give her a hug. "You didn't have to go with me. I wish you hadn't."

"We had to know if you needed help," Daphne replies. "But you're getting stronger."

"I'm getting madder," I say, barking a short laugh.

"That will fuel the strength," Millie says, taking each of our hands.

"I still don't know how to find him."

"In your dreams," Cash says. "And if that's what it takes to find him, we keep doing it."

"I need a break. But I can try again later."

"You deserve the break," Cash replies and kisses my forehead.

"We're not leaving here until this is over," Millie says. "Daphne and I will sleep here. We need to stick together. It's going to get more dangerous now. I don't know how I know that; I just do."

"Agreed." I nod and take a deep breath. "It's going to be dangerous. And fast."

Cash links his fingers with mine. "We're ready."

CHAPTER FIFTEEN

"I always seemed to enjoy everything that hurt."

~Albert Fish, AKA The Brooklyn Vampire

His balls feel heavy and swollen. They throb. That dumb bitch thinks she can hurt him, kick him, and then run away from him?

Fuck that. He'll teach her a lesson.

He'll teach them all a fucking lesson. She's losing her manners. Her respect for him. And he will not stand for that. No, he'll remind her just how important he is, how much she *loves* him.

Maybe she's forgotten how she used to look at him. How she played coy and hard to get. But he knew that was her way of flirting with him. He's stayed in the background for too long, given her too much independence.

It's time for that to change. Soon.

He paces his little house, back and forth, with throbbing balls and a bruised jaw. He showed her, didn't he? He took *two* women after she tried to hurt him, and he'll hurt them far more before he's done with them.

The anger fuels him. He stomps back to his room of pleasure and marches through the door, startling all five of his toys.

He knows it's not their fault. And taking *her* indiscretions out on them doesn't seem entirely fair, but he has energy to burn, and this is his favorite way to do that.

And...someone has to pay.

Someone *will* pay.

Dearly.

"Come here, Brielle."

He passes by the one that's been feisty. He doesn't have it in him to engage in a cat and mouse game tonight, and when he decides it's her time, he'll need more energy.

No, instead, he walks to one that he's only had a day or two and smiles into her sweet, precious face.

"You made me real mad tonight, Brielle."

Her face crumples, and she starts to cry, spit dripping down her chin as she begs and pleads with him to let her go.

"Oh, do you honestly think I will do that? That I

will let you go? Tsk tsk." He unties her from her restraints. "I won't let you go yet. You're still alive, silly girl."

She hiccups and keeps crying. She soils herself, which brings him great joy.

Yes, great joy, indeed.

"I don't think we'll play at the bench today." He kisses her cheek as he pulls her across the uneven wood floor to the chair. He saves the chair for special occasions.

Revenge feels like the perfect occasion.

He gets her situated, her hands and legs secured in the leather straps. Her mouth gapes soundlessly now, her despair palpable.

"You have to breathe, Brielle. It won't do to have you pass out on me now. That will only anger me. You don't want to anger me any more than you already have, do you?"

She shakes her head, but still, no sound emerges.

He grips her throat in his hand, squeezing slightly.

"I said breathe."

She takes a deep breath, her blue eyes pinned to his.

"Please don't kill me."

"I'm sorry, I'm going to have to disappoint you there."

He reaches for his favorite knife, but it's gone. Just one more thing to displease him today.

One more disappointment.

He chooses another blade, one not quite as sharp,

and then turns back to her. Without a word, he slices her flesh from hip to knee.

She keens in pain as the blood runs down the side of the chair.

"That will teach you not to run from me."

CHAPTER SIXTEEN

Cash

"It's good that I came," Felicia says into my ear. She arrived in Savannah this morning to check on my mom.

"What's going on?"

"Well, she hasn't been out of the house in a while," she says, speaking low. "And she's clearly not able to get around like she used to. The house hasn't been cleaned. Honestly, she needs help."

"We'll get her anything she needs. A housekeeper, a home nurse. Whatever she needs."

"Andy feels the same way, of course. And I agree. I just wanted to make sure I have your permission to make decisions and get things set up for her."

"Felicia, you know I trust you. Just keep us posted. And please tell Mom I love her."

"Will do. I'm going to take her to get her hair done and out for lunch today. We're having a girls' day."

"She'll love that. Thank you."

"Are you kidding? This is a vacation. Talk to you soon."

She ends the call just as Brielle walks out of the shower, wrapped in a fluffy, white towel.

"Was that Felicia?" she asks.

"Yes, she's at Mom's. It's good she's there. She will take care of things."

"She'll be great," Brielle says with a smile, but it doesn't reach her eyes. Her hand clutches her chest, and she scowls. "Why do I keep forgetting my pendant?"

She stomps back into the bathroom and calls out to me, "Have you seen my necklace?"

"You had it on this morning."

She pokes her head into the bedroom. "I know, and I took it off for my shower. Now, it's gone."

"Did you ask your sisters?"

She disappears again, and I hear her talking with her siblings.

"They haven't seen it," Brielle says as she bustles back into the bedroom and starts tearing the bed apart. "Maybe it came off while you were rocking my world."

"So, you're saying I rock your world?"

She rolls her eyes and looks at me like I'm ridiculous. "Maybe."

"On a scale of one to ten, where would I rank on the world-rocking scale?"

"Your ego is big enough without me feeding it, you know."

"Is my ego the only *big* thing I have?"

She barks out a laugh, the levity finally reaching her eyes. "You're silly."

I tug her to me and kiss her long and slow, reveling in how she fits against me as if she were made just for me.

"You two are disgusting," Daphne says from the doorway. "Millie and I are going to check out our respective businesses to make sure the sky hasn't fallen in either of them."

"We'll be back later," Millie calls from the hallway.

I kiss Brielle on the nose, and Daphne rolls her eyes then disappears down the hall.

"Bye!" Brielle calls with a laugh. "If I didn't know better, I'd say you enjoy taunting my sisters."

"Oh, I enjoy it very much," I confirm and nod. "I don't have to be in the office until around one today. Asher's working on a different case this morning."

"Perfect. Mallory called and asked if we'd like to have lunch with her and her husband, Beau."

I quirk a brow. "Beau Boudreaux? The tycoon?"

"One and the same." She nods and wanders to the closet to choose some clothes. "I haven't seen him in a long time. He's a busy guy."

"What with being a billionaire and all."

"And the owner of a massive company. He also has a big family. He's a nice guy. You'll like him."

"Okay," I reply and take her hand once she's dressed and ready to go. "Lead the way."

"I ADMIT," Beau says an hour later as we wait for our lunch to be served, "I'm fascinated by your career."

"It's not always as exciting as they portray it in the movies," I reply. "A lot of it is boring deskwork."

"But a lot of it isn't," Mallory replies. "And, I will say, I can't imagine having that much knowledge of how horrible human beings can be is an easy job. It must weigh heavily on you."

"Sometimes," I agree. "It depends on the job, of course. But you're right in that I don't necessarily work with the best of society."

"And now you're here, on your vacation, doing it again," Brielle says, taking my hand in hers and linking our fingers. "I'm sorry about that."

"I think I'm in the right place at the right time."

"That's a lovely way to think about it," Mallory says with a wide smile.

Our meals are served, and right after I've taken the first bite of my shrimp gumbo, my phone rings.

"I'm sorry. It's my boss in Dallas. I'd better take this."

I step away from the table, move out to the sidewalk, and accept the call.

"This is Winslow."

"It's Peters," he says, his voice brisk and all business. "I have news that you're not going to like, Cash."

I narrow my eyes. "What's up?"

"Simpson won't be going to prison."

There are moments in movies when the protagonist receives bad news, and the camera spins around them quickly as if everything is spiraling out of control.

This is that moment for me.

My stomach roils.

"Why the fuck not?"

"He's been found not guilty by reason of insanity. So, instead of a cage in prison, he'll be in a mental hospital for the rest of his life."

"Unacceptable. He's not fucking insane. I'll sit on the stand and testify."

"Too late," Peters says.

"Why wasn't I notified that this was going to trial? And how in the fucking hell did it happen so fast?"

"Your guess is as good as mine. I smell something dirty, but I can't prove it, and what's done is done."

"All of that work. For nothing?"

"He's going away," he reminds me. "Just not where you want him to go."

"I want him fucking dead." My voice is low and hard. "And I'd like to be the one to do it."

"I'm going to pretend I didn't hear that," Peters says. "Any news on the case you're working?"

"Nothing significant. I'll keep you posted."

"Do that."

He hangs up, and I squeeze the bridge of my nose, take a deep breath, and pull my shit together before walking back into the restaurant.

"Everything okay?" Brielle asks when I sit next to her.

"Fine." I clear my throat and reach for my water, wishing for something much stronger. Mallory's eyes narrow on me from across the table.

She's probably reading my mind. I have no idea how this stuff works, but I expect her to call me out on my lie.

Instead, she says, "Do you have siblings, Cash?"

"One brother. He's a cop here in New Orleans."

"Oh, that's awesome," she replies.

"My sister-in-law Kate's best friend is married to a cop," Beau says. "Asher Smith."

Brielle and I look at each other in surprise.

"Do you know him?" Beau asks.

"Actually, yes. We're working with him on a case," I reply.

"Well, he's a good man," Beau replies. "I trust him implicitly."

"I agree," Brielle says, surprising me. I actually got the feeling she didn't like Asher much. "I don't know him well, but he seems like a decent person and a good cop."

"How's that all going?" Mallory asks.

"Slow," I admit. "Frustratingly slow."

"It won't always," she says.

"If you know something about this, Mallory, I need you to tell me."

"I don't," she says, shaking her head. "I wish I did. I wish I could see it all clearly, but I only see flashes of things. Like Brielle, I see the dead. I'm a medium. And if I touch a person, I feel what they feel, and I can see their thoughts."

"That must be inconvenient," I say to Beau with a grin.

"I can't read him," Mallory says, leaning her head on Beau's shoulder. "It's one of the reasons I knew he was for me. But I assure you, if I knew the answers you seek, I'd tell you right away. What he's doing is pure evil."

"Thank you," I reply.

We spend another hour with small talk and finish our meals. After we've said goodbye to the other couple, Brielle and I set off for the police station. It's time for me to check in with Asher.

"What happened?" Brielle asks.

"To what?"

"You took that call, and when you came back, something was different. You covered it up well, but I know you well enough by now to see that something's off. What happened on that call? Is your mom okay?"

"It wasn't Felicia," I reply, taking a deep breath. It's time Brielle knew the truth of what happened before. Of the demons I carry. "It was Peters, my boss in Dallas, like I said."

"Do you need to go back to Texas?"

Her hand tightens on mine at the thought.

"No, he doesn't need me there. Do you remember when I told you that I'm here on a forced vacation?"

"Sure."

"I was assigned to a particularly difficult case in Maine six weeks ago. There was a killer up there, Rodney Simpson. He was taking men and sexually assaulting them, killing them, and then burying them in his backyard."

"Holy shit," she whispers.

"Statistically, a male serial killer who kills other men isn't that common. Yes, there are some out there—Dahmer, Gacy, the Candy Man, to name a few—but it's more commonly women or children, for many reasons that I won't bore you with right now. All we knew was that we had six men missing in Maine, and most likely a serial killer on our hands.

"The interesting thing was, he didn't just take men who were vacationing or on business from out of town. Yes, he did take a few of those, but he also snatched men who lived right there in the small town. When *that* happened more than once, it clued us all in that we likely had a multiple murderer.

"My unit was assigned, and we dug right in, finding more clues than local law enforcement had uncovered. Not because they did a bad job, we just had more experience and more tools at our disposal. I mean, a tiny town like that in Maine can rarely boast even a single murder, let alone something of that magnitude.

"It was frustrating, though, because he kept eluding

us. He was too calm and too detached to make a mistake."

"But he eventually made one, right?"

"Yes. Well, no, but he did get arrogant. He decided to start playing with us. He made us part of the game. He sent letters threatening the members of the team. Said he was going to take one of us and make an example of us. Of course, we took the threat seriously, but—"

"He *took* one of you?"

"Carlson," I confirm, feeling sick to my stomach. "He was forty-six, had been with the bureau for more than twenty years. A good man with a wife and five children. He went out to get us all coffee one morning and never came back."

"Oh my gods."

"He sent us video of what he was doing to Carlson." I swallow the bile and try to push the mental images from my mind. "I'll spare you the details. After four days of torture, he finally killed Carlson and left him strung up in the middle of Main Street in the dead of night."

"Didn't they have cameras?"

"Not before, no. This town was like going back in time thirty years. They didn't have any kind of security or surveillance before we got there. But it was one of the first things we did. The killer didn't know that we'd had them installed, and his public display cost him dearly. We got his identity."

"Who was it?"

I swallow again and stop when we get to the police station. We sit on a step, and I finish the story.

"Rodney Simpson. The chief of police."

"No way!"

"Yes, way. He was under our noses the entire fucking time, and we didn't know it. God only knows how many people he killed over the years. Maybe dozens. I spoke to him every single day. *Worked* with him. So did Carlson. And that's the really fucked-up thing. I don't know how I missed it. I don't know how I didn't figure it out sooner. *Six weeks*, Brielle, and that bastard didn't even trip my radar *one time*."

"It's not your fault."

She takes my face between her hands and makes me look into her eyes.

"The fact that that man is a sick bastard is not your fault. He's a monster, and he took a great deal of pleasure taunting all of you. I don't have to be psychic to know that. And you don't have to be a shrink to know that I'm right."

"Carlson died because I didn't do my job well or fast enough."

"No, he died because a person who swore to protect and serve turned out to be a psychopath, Cash. You know that as well as I do. You can't beat yourself up for that anymore, or it'll eat you up inside. Trust me on this."

"I don't want you to blame yourself for those girls' deaths, Bri."

"Any more than I want you to blame yourself for your friend's death. Sometimes, monsters walk among us, and there's just nothing we can do about that."

I kiss her hand and pull her to her feet.

"Let's go catch this particular monster, shall we?"

"Absolutely."

We walk into the building and go through the process of checking in at the reception desk. When we reach Asher's office, he jumps out of his chair and slides his phone into his pocket.

"You're just in time," he says. "We have another body."

We rush to the morgue in the basement of the building. Brielle's body tightens. I'm sure there are many spirits down here, ready to taunt the hell out of her.

"Are you okay?"

She nods stiffly. "I'm all right."

Asher opens the door to a cold room lined with freezers that hold bodies on rolling trays.

In the center of the room is a table holding a body with a sheet covering it.

"Pulled her from the swamp this morning," the medical examiner says. "Another swamp tour."

"He's getting sloppy," Asher says.

"Impatient," I reply. "He's working faster now. He's starting to make mistakes."

The ME glances at Brielle and then back to Asher. "She might not want to see this."

"I'm fine," Brielle says again.

"It's not pretty," he says as he grips the sheet and peels it down the corpse's torso.

"Oh," Brielle whispers, leaning over the body. "She wasn't tortured."

"Strangled," the ME confirms, pointing to the ligature marks around her neck. "She was definitely dead when she hit the water, though. No fluid in her lungs."

"That's unusual." Asher turns to me. "It doesn't follow the killer's MO."

"You're right." I narrow my eyes. "She does have dark hair, and it looks like she's about the right height."

"Sixty-seven inches," the ME says. We all look at him. "Five foot seven," he clarifies.

"But there are no other marks on her," Asher says. "Our guy is way angrier than this."

"Agreed." I glance down at Brielle. "Do you recognize her?"

"She's not one of the girls who's been following me," she says, shaking her head slowly. "I don't think I've seen her before."

"I'm not ready to rule this as a homicide," Asher says. "She might have killed herself."

"If she hung herself, how did she end up in the swamp?" I ask and notice Brielle pull her phone out of her purse. "What are you doing?"

"I want Daphne to touch her."

All of us turn to her in surprise.

"Who the hell is Daphne?" Asher asks.

"My sister," she responds. "She's psychic and psychometric, meaning she knows and sees things by touching objects. It works with people, too." Her attention turns to the phone call. "Hey, Daph? Can you come to the police station? It isn't going to be a fun visit. I need you to touch a dead body. I know. Are you sure? Okay, see you soon."

"I'm not sure I want a civilian touching my vic," Asher says.

"If she's not a victim, Daphne will know. And if she *is*, Daphne might be able to see the killer."

"I'll call up and tell them to escort her right down," Asher says immediately, making us both smile.

"Oh. While we wait, I should let you both know that I'm going back to work," Brielle says as casually as if she's talking about going to the grocery store.

"Negative, ghost rider." I shake my head emphatically. "Now that we know you're his target, you are absolutely *not* going to work."

"Cash, I need to try and lure him out. If he's really after me, if I'm his sick end game, I need to be somewhere that he can easily take me."

"No way."

"Actually, she's not wrong," Asher says. "And she won't be alone. We can have undercover officers on her tour. Hell, *you* can be on her tour. I'll go one night and take my wife and kids. We'll rotate. There will be eyes on her at all times."

"And eyes on everyone *around* me," she says. "If he's lurking nearby, there's a better chance that someone will notice him. I mean, he must be watching me, right?"

"What if this all blows up on us?" I ask desperately. "What if we do everything right, and he still manages to take you? I will not lose you to this sick asshole, Brielle. I'll protect you, no matter what it takes."

"I'm not Carlson," she says softly. "This is not the same thing. There are cameras in our town."

"Trust me, we've tried using them to find him," Asher says in disgust. "He must know where they are and has figured out how to evade them."

"He's smart," Brielle says. "But you said yourself, he's getting impatient. We need to end this. And doing that might just mean me putting myself out there as bait."

"This is a bad idea," I whisper. "And there will be rules. Strict rules, Brielle, I mean it."

"I won't do anything stupid," she says immediately. "Trust me, I don't want to get caught. But I do want to catch *him*."

Asher's phone rings. "Excellent. Bring her down."

"Is Daphne here?" Brielle asks.

"She's here."

CHAPTER SEVENTEEN

Brielle

"I can honestly say that no one's ever invited me to touch a dead body before," Daphne says when she walks through the door. She hugs me tightly before being introduced to Asher and then turns to the covered form on the table. "Let's get this over with."

"I want to reiterate what Brielle said," Cash says. "You don't have to do this."

"Are you kidding? I might see this bastard. Of course, I have to do this."

"Do you need her to be uncovered?" Asher asks.

"Yes, please." Daph takes a long, deep breath. She links her fingers with mine, and we silently recite our protection spell, the one we've used since we were small girls. When we open our eyes, the body is uncovered. "She wasn't tortured."

The surprise in Daphne's voice mirrors my own from earlier.

"That's why you're here," I say softly. "We need to know for sure if she was his victim."

"Lucky me," she whispers and licks her lips. She reaches out, her palm hovering over the girl's arm. As she touches her, skin to skin, she inhales sharply. "Oh, she was absolutely his."

"What do you see?" Cash asks.

"A lot, actually. Let me make some sense of it." She frowns, taking it all in. It's always been fascinating to watch Daphne *see*. Her eyes cloud over, her pupils dilate. "Okay, she was there a couple of days. She watched what he was doing to the others. She listened to them cry out, beg, sob. She didn't react much. And she knew that she wasn't going to let him do what he did to the others to her. So, when she was able to get her hands free of the ropes, she looped them over the bedpost and hung herself."

"Christ," Asher mutters, rubbing his hand over the back of his neck. "Can you see him?"

Daphne scowls. "Yes. I can see him. His back is to me, and he's sawing up a victim on his workbench."

"Has he turned around?" Cash asks.

"Not yet." Daphne pauses, and her breath hitches. "He's going to turn around. There he is. But..."

"But what?"

"I can't see his face. He's wearing a mask and something over his hair. Goggles."

"A disguise?" Asher asks.

"No, it's a surgical outfit," Daphne says. "Like he's

protecting a patient from his germs. It's so fucking creepy."

"Can you look for a different time?" I ask her. "Maybe when he took her?"

She shakes her head mournfully. "She's not showing me. She keeps showing me how she fell into the water. He dragged her by her arm. It dislocated her shoulder, and then he threw her over a railing into the water below."

"So he *lives* over water?" Asher says. "This is new information."

"I don't know if he lives there," Daphne replies. "But he's definitely holding the girls there. Because he just dragged her from the bed, outside, and hitched her over the rail, like I said. She's fading now."

"Fading?" Asher asks.

"Her spirit is weakening. She's leaving," Daphne says. "Everything loses its intensity over time, especially people, although I've never touched a corpse before. I usually get my information from *things*. Tables, chairs, a letter, a child's ball. I've never done this before. It feels like the end of a song when it fades away to nothing."

"So interesting," I whisper. "Thank you."

"I didn't do anything," she says as she backs away from the body and accepts a towel from the ME. "But I do know her name. Kathy Sikes. She was a mother. On vacation with a girlfriend just before her thirtieth birthday. She lived in Chicago."

"I'll find a way to reach her family," Asher says

quietly. "We may have a missing person report on her."

"You did a lot," I inform my sister. "You just helped Kathy rest peacefully. That will mean a lot to her and her family."

"I want to find this bastard," Daphne says, her voice strong with conviction. "I'm sick to death of his bullshit. Of him killing all these women. And why? Because they look like you? It's not fair."

"No, it's not," I agree and wrap my arm around her shoulders. "I wish I knew who the fuck this guy is, so we could find him and stop him."

We walk out of the morgue and take the elevator up to the first floor before stopping at the exit.

"I'm going with Daphne," I inform Cash and lean in to kiss his cheek. "We'll go find Millie. Daphne's shields are down now, and we need to get them restored, and I'm going to read through Grandma's book again. There *has* to be something in there that can help us stop this."

"I'll let you know when I'm done here," Cash says. "And, Brielle, don't you dare go back to work until I'm with you."

"I promise, I won't."

Daphne and I leave the police station and turn toward Witches Brew.

"You're going back to work?" she asks casually.

"I have to. I have to lure this fucker out."

"That's probably dangerous."

We walk a full city block in silence before she speaks again.

"He doesn't hate you," she says, surprising me.

"Who?"

"The killer. He's not doing this because he hates you."

I stop on the sidewalk and turn to her. "How do you know that?"

"Because *he* touched *her* and I could feel that. He doesn't think he's acting out of anger. In fact, he loves you. Or at least he believes he does."

"That's beyond fucked-up, even for a serial killer."

"Hey, I'm no profiler, and it was a super brief impression, but when he took her, when he touched her, he felt happiness. Affection."

"I don't have many men in my life." The frustration hangs heavily in my voice. "I have Cash. That's pretty much it. On a regular basis, anyway."

"Well, he knows you. And, no, I don't know how or why. If I did, I would have said so back there. It's so damn frustrating."

We walk into Witches Brew and stop short.

"You're kidding," Daphne says as a smile spreads over her face.

"A little help?" Millie asks, trying to control a coffee machine that seems to be going crazy, all by itself.

"What in the world?"

We hurry behind the counter and start flipping knobs and switches, but it doesn't help. Finally, I crawl under the bar and unplug the machine entirely, and everything goes quiet.

"Thank you," Millie says. She's wiping her brow when I shimmy out and sit on my ass, right there in a puddle.

"What did you do?" I ask.

"It was just a little spell I've been working on," she says with a shrug. "I thought it would be nice if the machine worked a little faster, but I must have said something wrong because—"

"Because it went crazy like something out of *Beauty and the Beast*?" Daphne asks, her hands on her hips.

"Well, yeah." Millie sighs. "Sorry, guys. I'll clean this up."

"We'll help." I stand, and the three of us mop up the milk and water as Daphne and I fill our sister in on the happenings of the past hour.

"You've been busy," Millie says softly. "I'm sorry, Daph."

"It could be worse," Daphne says. "I could have dead people following me around the city."

Both of them turn to me. "How many now?" Millie asks.

"Six." I sigh and glance out the window to the sidewalk. "He killed someone last night. They just follow me. Sometimes, their mouths move like they're speaking, but I can't hear them. It's frustrating as hell."

"The answer is in the dream-walking," Millie says.

"How do you know?" I ask.

"Because you never dream-walked before this. It's new. And because no one is going to find him without you seeing where he is or *who* he is. It's up to you, and I hate that for you, but I also kind of think it makes you a serious badass."

"I mean, I *am* a badass," I agree with a grin. "And I hate that it's up to me because I feel like I'm failing."

"I don't even want to suggest this," Daphne says, "but I think you need to fully surrender yourself to it. Let your shields down completely when you go to sleep."

"No," Millie says, horrified.

"It's the best way," I agree, thinking it over. "If I keep protecting myself, it's less likely that I'll see everything I need to. I'm missing things. Daphne's right."

"We'll be with you, as always," Daphne reassures us.

"Right now." I stand and reach for my bag. "I want to do it right now."

"You're just going to force yourself to go to sleep?" Millie asks.

"You can give me something to make me sleep."

"It makes you so damn groggy, we'll be lucky if you wake up by Thursday."

"It's only Monday," Daphne says in surprise.

"Exactly," Millie agrees.

"So, give me a smaller dose." I shrug. "But whip it up fast because we're heading back to my apartment."

"You'd better give Cash a heads-up," Daphne warns. "I don't want to be on his shit list."

"Are you afraid of Cash?" I ask, surprised.

"No, but he's going to be around for a long time, and

I want him to like me." She smiles smugly.

"How do you know that?"

"Oh, please," Millie says as she measures something with a special spoon. "We don't have to be psychic to see that the man is completely in love with you."

"It's weird, isn't it? We were thrown together because of a serial killer, and we're falling in love."

"There are weirder ways to fall in love," Daphne points out. "It could be in prison or something."

"You're not helping."

———

"YOU'RE BACK."

Sarah's sitting on her little bed.

"You're still here."

"Damn right, I am." She smiles thinly but it doesn't reach her tired eyes. "It's happening faster now, though. So many girls...gone."

"Why hasn't he hurt you?" I wonder aloud.

"Because I fight back, and I think that scares him. Or excites him." She hitches a shoulder. "And I'm gonna keep fighting back."

"Do you still have the knife?"

"Yep. He was mad when he couldn't find it. Sick fuck."

I nod and glance around. At least one more girl I don't recognize. Maybe two.

"He's taking so many now."

"And killing them faster," she agrees.

"I'm going to try to go out there now. I have to see him. I have to figure out where we are so I can bring the police here. We're working really hard, Sarah. I promise."

She only nods as I walk to the door and try the knob.

This time, to my utter surprise, it gives.

I can walk out the door!

It opens to a hallway, with the smell of pine hanging in the air. As if someone came through with a cheap can of aerosol air-freshener and doused everything with it.

He must be covering the smell from the room.

I gingerly walk down the hallway. Nobody should be able to hear or see me, but Sarah can, so I'm not taking any chances.

I can hear music playing. Soft strains that sound like something from the '40s. Big band-style, but slow. It's the only nice thing I've seen or heard in this place.

The floor creaks under my foot, and I stop, waiting to see if anyone comes running around the corner.

No one does.

I pass one open doorway and glance inside, then have to fight off the urge to throw up.

It's a shrine. A fucking shrine with candles and flowers and incense burning.

And a picture of ME in the middle.

He's made a shrine to me.

Who the hell is this sick bastard?

I back away and keep going down the hall. On the left is another open door with another shrine.

But it's not my photo in the center.

It's Millie.

The air whooshes out of me as I back away and come to
another room, this time with a shrine built around a photo of
Daphne.

So, it's not just me he's after.

It's all of us.

The living room is neat as a pin. The furniture is old with
holes and faded fabric, but the pillows are placed precisely in
the corners. The green shag carpet has recently been vacuumed.

Footsteps in the kitchen grow louder as someone walks my
way, and I stiffen, hoping with all my might that I recognize
him and that he doesn't know I'm here.

He doesn't look at me as he walks past, so close that I can
smell him. I can feel the heat coming off his body.

Suddenly, I realize I do know him. I do recognize him.

I didn't even know he was still alive.

"Oh, hello," he says as he looks at me and gives me a happy,
wide smile. "Brielle! You're here. I'm so happy to see you."

I look around, wanting to escape, forgetting that I'm in a
dream.

It's a dream.

"Yes, I can see you. I can always see you." He smiles kindly.
"Did you see my room of fun?" He gestures to the back of the
house where the girls are. "Isn't it great? I've been doing all of
this for you, of course. I just knew you'd love it. I've been
waiting for you because I wanted to have enough practice to
make everything perfect for you.

"You're special, Brielle."

He laughs and looks around his house.

"I'm so glad I cleaned up this morning so the house was nice *for you. Now, I know what you're thinking..."*

He holds up his hands in surrender and sits in an old chair in the corner. I haven't said a word yet, haven't even confirmed that I am, in fact, here.

"You're wondering why I would do such special things for you and not your sisters. After all, fair's fair, right? Well, I have so many wonderful things planned for them, too, don't you worry. But you're the oldest, Brielle, so it just made sense to start with you. They'll understand, won't they?"

I don't reply. I simply tilt my head, watching him quietly. I remember him well, but I don't ever remember him speaking this much. I didn't even know he could talk this much. I always assumed he was stupid. I never liked him. He always gave me the heebie-jeebies.

Guess I was right to listen to those instincts.

"Brielle?" He frowns as he watches me. "Aren't you going to say anything?"

"I don't know what to say." And if that's not the truth, I don't know what is. I don't want to set him off, to send him into an angry tirade and have him go off and kill all of the girls in that room.

But I also don't want to encourage him.

I'm no psychiatrist!

"Brielle." He stands and walks to me, taking my shoulders in his hands, and I want to throw up again. I do not want his hands on me.

I never did. Just a brush of his hand on my shoulder when I was a kid made me shiver.

And I'm not sure why he can touch me in this dream when

I can't touch anything.

"I'm sure you're so overwhelmed with excitement that you don't know what to say. I understand. You've always been such a sweet girl."

"You barely know me," I whisper.

"I admit, it's been a while, but I know everything, *Brielle. I've watched you on your little tour. You're such a smart woman, aren't you? I know you've decided to date that man. Now, I admit, I didn't like it. I wanted to just cut his head right off his body the first time I saw you two together. But I also knew it was just a matter of time until you came around."*

"Came around to what?"

"Well, that we're all meant to be together, of course. Just the way it was supposed to be all along."

"You're crazy."

The words are out of my mouth before I can stop them. His expression falls. The look in his eyes hardens. But before he can do anything else, I smile.

"You're crazy to think that I wouldn't *want that too, of course."*

"There now," he says, satisfied. "That's a good girl."

I wake with a start and run to the bathroom, then hover over the toilet and throw up until my body is wracked with dry heaves. I can't stop it. Someone rubs my back while someone else sets a cool rag on my neck.

Finally, I sit on my haunches and look up to find Daphne, Millie, and Cash all staring down at me with concern.

"I know who he is."

CHAPTER EIGHTEEN

"After my head has been chopped off, will I still be able to hear, at least for a moment, the sound of my own blood gushing from my neck? That would be the best pleasure to end all pleasure."
-Peter Kurten, AKA the Vampire of Dusseldorf

He hasn't been this excited in a long time. Brielle finally knows what his plans are, and despite it coming earlier than he anticipated, he's pleased.

Yes, they will have to decide what her punishment will be for jumping the gun. The timeline is there for a reason, and she ignored it. That displeases him, so there will be consequences for that.

Should he cut out her tongue? He ponders that for a moment as he sharpens his second-favorite knife in the corner of the room of pleasure. No, cutting out her tongue would mean he could no longer have wonderful conversations with her, and that would be a pity.

Perhaps he should just take her toes. They are pretty little digits, but she has displeased him, and that means she needs to be punished.

Losing those pretty little toes will be a great punishment indeed.

Satisfied with his plan, he turns to the girls. The new ones are too fresh. Their fear too raw. They certainly won't do for today's fun. He needs one of the seasoned girls.

His eyes move to the one on the end, the one he's kept the longest of any of the girls he's taken. He's not sure why he decided to draw out the inevitable for her. She still has a lot of spirit, which he admits, he admires.

He's enjoyed having her here, but it's time for her to have some fun.

She's earned it, after all.

"Oh, Brielle, today has been such a treat." He whistles to himself for a moment as he gets his workstation ready for her. He's decided to treat himself even more today and play with the disemboweling again. He so enjoyed it the last time, although he got too excited and his toy died before he was able to fully detach her anus from her body.

It really was disappointing. But this time, he'll be more careful. He's been practicing in his head, running it over and over, and he's certain he won't make the same mistakes again.

The table is freshly cleaned, and his tools are ready when he turns to the girl with a smile.

"Today is very special indeed, Brielle. We are going to have *so* much fun. Now, I'll wait to put my gear on until after I get you situated. I know that's not how I usually go about things, but I honestly enjoy the way your little body feels against mine without the rubber apron. And soon, not today, but very soon, we're going to be together in the *most* special way, so I'll let myself feel you today."

She doesn't flinch. She's not breathing hard. She looks calm and collected and resigned to what's about to happen.

It's the most beautiful thing he's ever seen.

It's as if she loves him as much as he loves her.

Finally!

"Okay, Brielle." He leans over and unties her hands, then helps her to a standing position and starts to turn toward the bench. Suddenly, the unthinkable happens.

His knife, his favorite knife, is suddenly plunged into his side, right into his stomach. He stares at her, pain rushing through him.

"I told you I was going to kill you, you sick fuck."

He slaps her hard, sending her to the ground, and pulls the knife out of his side. Blood spurts over his hand covering the wound.

"Brielle," he keens. "How could you?"

He starts to cry, shaking his head.

So much blood.

And he's so sad. She hurt him! She tried to kill him.

No. Not his Brielle.

She wouldn't do that.

This one is no good.

He has to stop the bleeding.

"Ruth," he mutters as he hurries out the back door and down the stairs that lead to solid ground. "Ruth can stop it."

He hasn't seen her in a while, but she wouldn't turn him away, not when he's like this. She'll help him stitch up the wound, and then he'll go back and kill that little bitch.

How could she?

How *dare* she?

He trips and falls to the ground, his shoe falling off in the process. He stares down at it.

Should he try to put it back on? There are so many things in the swamp that could hurt his feet.

His mama always told him that.

But there's no time. Too much blood.

He wrestles his way back to his feet and shuffles along. The house is only a mile from his. He could get there blindfolded.

Yes, this is the right thing.

Ruth will help.

But he's sweating in the heat, and he's lost so much blood. Too much. It's running down his side, his leg. Everything is going dark around the edges of his vision.

Why is he so cold?

He needs Ruth to put a blanket on him, that's all. She has lots of blankets.

But maybe he'll stop in this old shed and take a break. Just to catch his breath, then he can make it the rest of the way to Ruth's house.

He hobbles inside and slides to the ground.

Critters have made this their home over the years. The roof is gone. He can't escape the hot sun.

And as he closes his eyes, he knows he won't make it to Ruth's.

Suddenly, he's hovering over his body. There's so much blood. There's no way he can survive.

But that doesn't mean he can't finish the job he's set out to do. It's still the most important thing, after all.

And now that he's free of that worthless, aging body, he can work even more diligently.

He soars over his old house, past the driveway, and onto the road leading to the highway.

Then he floats down to the road.

And waits.

CHAPTER NINETEEN

Cash

"Who is he?" I demand, my heart hammering in my ears.

"Horace."

The girls all stare at each other. "What?" Daphne asks at last.

"It's Horace," Brielle repeats and stands to walk back to the bedroom. "And he's a fucking psychopath. Call Asher."

"On it." I dial the other man's number and as soon as he answers, I start talking. "She knows who he is. First name is Horace. What's his last name?" I ask.

"I have no idea," Daphne says with a frown. "He was always just Horace."

"We know where he lives," Millie says. "Right by Mama."

"Jesus. Did you hear that?"

"I heard it," Asher says, "but I don't know what it means."

"I'll send you the address of their mother's house. If Horace is nearby, he can't be far. We're headed there now."

"We're leaving, too. Give me that address. And, Cash, follow protocol. We don't want anything to mess up this bust."

I text him the address while we hurry down to the car. I'm driving, with Brielle in the passenger seat. "Now, who the hell is Horace?"

"He was a man who lived near us growing up," Brielle says. She pulls on her bottom lip, watching the city speed by. "Our parents hired him here and there to help around the house. He did yard work, painted the house, did some plumbing, electrical. Really, he was the family handyman."

"Creepiest handyman ever," Millie mutters from the back seat. She grabbed their grandmother's book on the way out of the apartment and is now reading it in her lap. "I never liked that guy."

"None of us did," Daphne agrees.

"Why? What made him so creepy?"

"He was just always *there*," Brielle says. "If we were outside playing, he was nearby, trimming hedges or pruning flowers. If we were inside watching TV, he was just beyond the window, looking in."

"Did he ever approach you? Touch you?" My

stomach turns at the thought of some sick fuck putting his hands on these women when they were girls.

"No, he never touched us," Daphne says. "In fact, he avoided touching us. I remember one time, he was sitting at the table in the kitchen having coffee with Mama, and I walked past him and innocently brushed his arm. He recoiled as if I'd burned him."

"He and Mama had an affair for years," Brielle adds. "She played with him. I was a kid, and still I knew it. She used to laugh when he left the house."

"They weren't quiet," Millie says. I glance at her in the rearview and watch her wince. "And she humiliated him. Even back then, I knew it. Why in the world would he come back for more of that nonsense?"

"Could be a pattern for him," I reply, thinking it over. "If his mother humiliated him, and then *your* mother did the same, he might think that that's how women behave. That it's normal."

"Well, that's just fucked-up," Daphne says.

"I mean, he's a serial killer," Brielle reminds them. "So, pretty much everything he does is fucked-up."

Lights flash behind me just as my phone rings.

"Asher," I say into the phone.

"We're behind you. I have four more cars behind *me.*"

"Excellent," I reply. "Just follow me. The road in there is rough, so it'll be slow going once we're off the main road. I'd say we're about twenty minutes away."

"Copy that. Once we get to the house, you do *not* go inside."

"I know the procedure," I reply and hang up. "I'm with the FBI for fuck's sake."

Brielle reaches over and takes my hand in hers, giving it a squeeze. I glance her way and smile.

This is almost over.

I'm so fucking relieved. I want to be with her in a normal setting when I'm not constantly worried about her well-being. I just want to *be* with her.

"We're almost there," Daphne says, pointing to the lane that turns off the main road. "Turn there. After we go over that part that was washed out, turn right. His house is about a half a mile from the turn."

"Got it."

We have to slow down more than I'd like, but there's no choice with the lane in the condition it's in.

Just when I round a bend, Brielle holds up a hand.

"Stop the car."

"What?"

"Stop the goddamn car."

I slam on the brakes and turn to stare at her. "What? What is it?"

"Do you see him?"

She's staring straight ahead. I follow her gaze and about come out of my skin.

Standing maybe ten feet in front of the car is a shadow.

A man.

"I fucking see him," I mutter in surprise.

"He's dead," Brielle says.

"Do you see a shadow or a man?" Millie asks. "Because I see a shadow."

"Me, too," Daphne says.

"That makes three of us," I add.

"I see a man. I see Horace," Brielle says. "Drive through him."

"Are you sure?"

"Oh, yeah. Fuck him."

I nod once, put the car in drive, and step on it, plowing right through the shadow. It dissipates around us, and I gingerly drive over the washed-out area, then turn onto Horace's driveway.

Sure enough, about a half-mile later, a small house comes into view. The back side of it butts up to the swamp and has a rickety porch suspended over the expansive water beyond it. The house is small, and it leans to one side. But the roof has been recently patched.

I stop the car and wait while Asher and his men jump out of their vehicles and surround the house, all of them armed.

Less than three minutes after they break down the door, Asher comes out and gestures for us to follow him.

"He's not here," he says as we walk through the front door. "But we found the women, all still alive."

"Whoa." Millie's eyes are wide as she stands in the

living room and stares at the photos on the walls. "It's all three of us."

"He told me that we were all part of his stupid plan. I was just first because I'm the oldest," Brielle says and takes Millie's hand in hers. "He had plans for you and Daph, too, but he didn't say what they were."

"I killed him." The girl's the first to be escorted out, wrapped in a blanket. "At least, I think I did. I stabbed him, and then he hit me and ran away. But there's no way he could survive that. I stabbed him in the gut."

"Get men out to the swamp," Asher orders one of his men. "We're going to find that fucker."

"Sarah." Brielle approaches the other woman carefully. "Do you remember me?"

Glassy eyes turn to Brielle, and then Sarah starts to cry.

"You found us," she says and wraps her arms around Brielle. "I did what you said. I stabbed him."

"You are a fucking badass, Sarah Chandler. I'm so damn proud of you."

"We all are," Daphne says, joining in on the hug. Millie wraps her arms around all of them, and they stand for a long moment, giving each other comfort and strength.

And if I know these girls at all, they're adding a little magic to the mix right now for Sarah, as well.

Once all the abducted girls are loaded into ambulances and taken to the hospital, I join Asher back in the killer's playroom.

I stop at the doorway and take it all in. I've seen other lairs, and I've seen more blood, but I don't know if I've seen this level of absolute *evil*.

Three toddler-sized beds line one wall, each with a bare, soiled mattress. An electric chair is in the corner, and the opposite wall boasts the biggest workbench I've ever seen in my life, with tools of all shapes and sizes lining shelves above the bench. They've all been cleaned, but forensics will lift blood samples from the tools and the counter. And, most likely, the floor, beds, and chair.

"Fucking hell," Asher says, his hands on his hips as he stares at dozens of brunette braids hung on the wall. "Thirty-six."

"He's killed far more than that," I reply as I join him.

"Why didn't he keep more trophies?"

"Oh, he most likely did. We'll probably find them all somewhere in this house. These are just the trophies he was admiring for killing Brielle."

Asher turns to me. "How are you able to stomach this?"

"I won't lie to you, this one isn't easy because it *is* Brielle, and she's mine. No case is a walk in the park, but this one makes me want to kill him with my bare hands. That doesn't happen often."

"We're searching the house as we speak, so we'll discover anything else there is to find. Did you see the shrines in the bedrooms?"

"Yeah." I swallow hard. "He's apparently been obsessed with them since they were kids. They grew up in a house about a mile from here, and Brielle told me he used to be their handyman and that he had an affair with their mother."

"Sick fuck," Asher says.

"We found something!"

Both Asher and I hurry to the master bedroom where a team has been searching.

"I pulled up this rug, and sure enough, there was a hole cut in the floor," Officer Thibideaux says. "And I found this."

He points to the box sitting on the bed. It's made of wood and has something sculpted into the lid.

"It's a star," I say, staring down at it.

"It's a pentagram." I spin at Brielle's voice behind me. "I couldn't figure out why he could see me when I was dream-walking, or how he could touch me in the dream. I'm pretty sure Sarah's sensitive and may not know it, and that's why *she* could see me. But him? I couldn't figure it out at first.

"But after being here, in his house, and having my own shields down somewhat, I know. Not only is he psychic, but he's also a witch. That's a pentagram. I don't know how long he's been practicing. I don't know how powerful he was or where he learned his craft. I don't know if he comes from a line of witches. But I'll start doing some research and ask around. But you all need to know before you open that box that it most likely has a protective spell on it, and it may have a booby trap hex, as well."

"A *booby trap hex*?" Asher asks, a smirk appearing. "Is that the official term?"

"No, the official term is it could burn your hand off if you touch it. Does that help?"

Thibideaux shakes his head and reaches for the box. When a bolt of lightning shocks his hand, he backs right off in surprise.

"How do we open it, then?" Asher asks.

Millie walks into the room, takes a deep breath, and smiles. "Because the one who cast the spell is dead, I can break it. Give me some room, please."

We all stand back and watch with rapt attention as she splays her hands over the box, looks up to the sky, and begins to chant.

"Lord and Lady working for me and through me, assist me in breaking the spell cast on this object. The wielder has passed beyond the veil and no longer holds sway over this object or its contents. For the good of all, according to free will, grant me access, and—"

I don't really hear all of the words she says after that. The room grows warm, and light fills the space, and then it's gone in a flash as Millie sighs deeply.

"There, it's safe."

Asher reaches for the box, and nothing happens to his hands when he removes the lid.

"Cash."

I join him and feel my jaw tighten at what's inside.

"Looks like he had a thing for eyeballs," Asher says quietly.

There must be a hundred eyeballs in the box.

"Get this to the ME," Asher says. "I want to know how many there are. If he took both of his victims' eyes, or just one. I want to know *everything* about this son of a bitch."

I walk out of the room and lead all three sisters out of the house. They all look exhausted.

"They haven't found his body yet," Millie says and turns to Daphne. "Were you able to pick anything up on him?"

"I touched things in there," Daphne says, her voice trembling slightly. "All I saw were echoes. Memories. Nothing from the present."

"He's here," Brielle says, looking down at her feet. "He's been following us through the house, grinning. He's proud of his work."

"If that isn't the creepiest thing I've ever heard, I don't know what is," Millie says.

"I mean, there *were* at least a hundred eyeballs in a box, so there's that, too," Daphne reminds her. "I don't want him following Bri for the rest of her life. We need to get rid of him."

"He's not going to stay," Brielle says in surprise. She's looking at something, or someo*ne*, in front of her. "He just said goodbye."

"Just like that?" Millie asks and turns to me. "What are the chances that a serial killer would be like, '*well, you got me. Peace out!'?"*

"Slim to none," I agree with her. "But I won't complain if that's his plan."

"Me either," Daphne says, just as two of the men who set off to look for the body come running back to the house.

"What do you have?" I ask.

"We found his shoe and a large pool of blood on the ground right next to the swamp."

"We think he collapsed there and was dragged away by a critter," the other officer says.

"Keep looking," Asher says from the doorway. "We'll keep searching for his body until dark, and then we'll look again tomorrow."

"He's dead," Brielle says.

"You and your sisters keep saying that, but I don't see a body, and without that, I can't confirm that he's gone. I can't tell all of those families that my psychic consultant assures me he's dead, so it must be true."

"I know," Brielle says with a shrug. "I get it. But he can't hurt anyone anymore, and that's the most important thing."

I wrap my arm around her shoulder and pull her against me so I can kiss her temple. "Proud of you," I whisper in her ear.

"I want all of you to go home," Asher says, pointing to us. "Cash, I'll need you at the office this evening for a full debriefing, and possibly the news conference.

Reporters will ask questions I may not be able to answer."

"Just let me know when and where you need me," I assure him.

"I want to go to the hospital to see the girls," Brielle says. "They need some strength today."

"We'll all go," Daphne says. "Millie, let's stop by the Brew and make them some potions."

"Excellent idea," Millie says, heading for the car. "Let's go."

Once the girls are in the vehicle waiting for me, I turn back to Asher.

"I have plenty to say about this animal, but I didn't want to say it in front of those three. He's not a typical psychopath. I'll brief you more later."

"Agreed," Asher says and nods. "I've never seen *anything* like this, and I've been in homicide for a long fucking time. I'd like to hear your thoughts. Go take care of the women, and I'll see you in a few hours."

I nod, and once I'm in the car and headed back toward the city, Brielle turns to me.

"What did you say to him once we were out of earshot?"

I take her hand and kiss her knuckles. "That, darlin', is none of your business."

"Well, he told you," Millie says and laughs. "I can't believe I can laugh after what we just saw. He had *shrines*. With photos and everything."

"Where did he get the snapshots?" Daphne

wonders. "They're pictures even Mama wouldn't have because they were clearly taken after we left."

"Unfortunately," Brielle says with a sigh, "I think we're going to have to go to Mama's at some point and ask some questions."

"Why?" Millie asks.

"Because she's his *neighbor* and has known him for as long as I can remember. She'll know something more than we do."

"She doesn't know who *we* are these days," Daphne says. "How do you expect her to know anything about Horace killing innocent women?"

"It's worth a try," Brielle insists. "But not today. We've all been through enough. I'm just relieved that it's over. He can't hurt anyone else."

"Is he still following you?" Millie asks.

"No, and the murdered girls are gone, too. They were gone as soon as we stepped out of my apartment after my dream. I'm telling you, it's over. We can all go back to living our lives."

"Well, thank the goddess for miracles," Millie says. "Now, let's go take care of those girls."

CHAPTER TWENTY

Brielle

N o one follows me around for the first time in
weeks, and I'm ridiculously happy about it.

No creepy dead girls.

No Horace.

Just the usual shadows of New Orleans here and
there. Surprisingly, they don't scare me like they used to.
There are more shadows in the hospital, which is to be
expected.

I'm easily able to ignore them.

"I hope they let us in soon," Millie says, holding a
tray of hot chocolates, each containing a spell of protection and healing. "I don't want these to get cold."

"You can come back," a nurse says from the doorway
leading to the ER rooms. "All of the ladies are awake
and would like to say hello."

"Are you sure?" Daphne asks. "They've been through
something pretty horrible."

"They have family with them and will be here for a couple of days. But, yes, they agreed to see you."

We stop at each room, offering a cup of hot chocolate and lots of hugs.

"I look like you," the one named Megan says softly. "You're so lucky he didn't take you."

"I know I am." I nod and push away the sudden guilt that pierces my heart. It's not my fault, and I know that, but I can't help but feel responsible for the suffering that these girls endured.

I can't imagine the fear, the horror.

I purposefully save my visit with Sarah for last. My sisters don't join me when I walk into the room. Sarah's face lights up when she sees me. "Hey!"

"Hey, yourself." I sit on the bed near her hip. "How do you feel?"

"A little better now that they're pumping some fluids into me," she says, pointing to her IV. "I'm happy to have all of my brothers here. I might not let them out of my sight again."

"The feeling's mutual, squirt."

I turn to look at Sarah's brothers and feel my eyes widen. They're all big men, well over six feet, with broad shoulders and meaty hands.

I wouldn't want to piss any of them off.

"It's nice to meet you all."

"Sarah says you came to her sometimes and talked to her," one of the brothers says with a frown. "How is that even possible?"

"I don't know for sure." I shrug and shake my head. "I was dream-walking. And if I told you everything, you'd think I'm crazy."

"No, I think the dick that did this is crazy," he replies. "I'm grateful to you for helping Sarah escape."

"Sarah did that because she's a badass. She has older brothers who taught her how to take care of herself. I was just there at the right moment when a knife had been left on the floor and pointed it out."

"Either way, we're grateful," another brother says. "We're going to go get something from the cafeteria while you two talk."

"Thanks."

Sarah sighs. "It feels like a nightmare. I mean, I know I'm starving and dirty and my muscles hurt from sitting on that fucking bed, but part of me feels like it was all a long, drawn-out night terror."

"Worst nightmare ever," I reply softly. "So, you remember seeing me?"

"You were standing in that room as clearly as you're here right now," she says. "It confused the hell out of me. I thought I was imagining things at first, but then you talked to me. I figured, even if I was going crazy, having someone to talk to was kind of nice."

"Have you ever considered yourself sensitive to paranormal things?" I ask, watching her carefully.

"Sure. I grew up in a haunted house. Nothing too crazy, just footsteps here and there. I don't see dead people, like that movie, but I've checked into hotels and asked to have my room changed because the one they gave me felt off. That sort of thing. Is that what you mean?"

"That's exactly what I mean," I confirm. "I think that's why you were able to see me, and the others weren't. Sarah, I'm so sorry for what you went through, what you must have witnessed in that place."

"I closed my eyes a lot of the time," she admits on a whisper. "And I feel like a damn wimp for it, but I think I would have really gone out of my mind if I'd watched, you know?"

"Absolutely."

"He was a monster."

"The worst kind there is," I agree. "But he's gone. You got him."

"Did they find his body yet?"

I frown and check my phone. There's no message from Cash. "I don't know. They hadn't yet when we left the scene earlier, but I haven't heard anything since then. They might have."

"What if they don't? What if I didn't kill him after all, and he's off somewhere getting stitched up?"

"He's not." I clear my throat. "Sarah, I'm psychic. A medium. I *do* see dead people. And I saw him. He's dead, and that won't change whether they find his body or not."

"Wow." She swallows hard. "Well, that sucks for you."

We're quiet for a moment, both lost in our own

thoughts, and then it's like a light bulb goes off in her head.

"Wait. Does that mean that you could see the others? The other women?"

"Yeah. I could see them. That's how I knew something was going on. They came to me to warn me, and to tell me to find them. But now that he's gone, they're gone, too."

"Well, I think that sucks just as much for you as it does for the rest of us." She reaches for my hand and grips it fiercely. "You're a victim, too."

"We're not victims, Sarah. We're still here."

"Damn right, we are. Can we stay friends? I mean, I know it sounds weird, and if it's too off the wall for you, that's okay, I just—"

"We're totally friends," I say, interrupting her. "I'd like that very much."

I DON'T THINK a shower ever felt so good. I bet that's how the others felt today once they knew they were safe and were able to wash away the filth from their time in that horrible room.

Best shower ever.

I hope that all the girls get the best counseling there is, and that they're able to heal from their ordeal.

I towel-dry my hair then twist it up into a bun and dry off the rest of my body. When I reach for the lotion, I see my necklace, sitting right there by the sink as if it was there all along.

I searched high and low for it this morning and couldn't find it.

"Must be going blind in my old age," I mutter as I smooth lotion on my legs and loop the chain over my neck. "Apparently, thirty is when it all goes downhill."

I smirk and pad out of the bathroom. My sisters both went home tonight, ready to get back to their lives. Part of me misses them already. We've always been close—except for my spat with Daphne—and it's been nice having them nearby these past couple of weeks.

Having Daph speaking to me again is the best thing ever.

But I know they're not far away, and I'll most likely see one or both of them tomorrow.

I pause at the doorway of my bedroom and smile when I see Cash sitting up in bed, waiting for me.

Speaking of the best thing ever.

"Hey there," I say as I walk to the side of the bed and slip between the covers next to him.

"Hey, yourself."

"How are you?"

"I think this might be the most tired I've ever been in my entire life," he says with a gusty sigh. "But it feels good to know *he's* gone and not coming back, and that everyone's safe tonight."

"Yeah." I cozy up next to him, enjoying the way it feels when he wraps his arm around me, and I fit right under his shoulder. I can hear his heart beating. "I like that, too. The whole thing is weird, don't you think?"

"The fact that you saw murder victims and we tracked down the killer, only to discover that he had a thing for you and your sisters? Whatever do you mean?"

"Smartass." I snort. "There are some holes that need to be filled, though."

"I don't want to talk about this tonight, Brielle."

I look up at him. "You don't?"

"No. We've been talking about it for weeks, and now that it's over, I want to take one night to just enjoy you. We can talk about it tomorrow."

"I mean, I'm right here, just waiting to be enjoyed."

He pushes me onto my back and takes a tour of my shoulders with his lips. Tingles float over my skin, making me feel more alive than ever before.

Each time we're together, it's better than the last. I don't even know how that's possible.

"I love your skin," he murmurs before catching a nipple with his lips. "So soft, so pink."

I push my fingers through his hair, happy to let him lazily work his way across my flesh. He's not an impatient man when it comes to sex. He likes to linger, enjoy, and it makes my toes curl.

I've never met anyone like him. And I know that there will be no one like him ever again.

So I lie back and enjoy the lazy, sexy ride.

"This is the Andrew Jackson Hotel." I point behind me and smile at my group. Oh, my goddess, it feels good to be back at work. I didn't realize how much I loved this job until I couldn't be here for a while. "This was an all-boys school, way back in the day."

I talk about the school burning down, and how the boys are said to still be there, haunting the halls.

This group has been lively, with a few more hecklers than usual, but a few quick-witted comebacks from me seems to have calmed them down for the most part.

"We're staying there," a man says, making me smile.

"Someone on my tour always is." I wink and lead them farther down the street, giving them little details about specific buildings. Not all of them are haunted, some of them are just interesting because of how old they are and what may or may not have taken place there once upon a time.

The best part of the tour this evening is that there are no new shadows. Nothing different at all tonight, and that makes me happiest of all. The girls are truly at rest, and we're ready to get on with our lives.

To go back to *normal*. Whatever that is.

"How do you know all this stuff?" a guy asks as we walk down the sidewalk. "Are you psychic or something?"

"What would you say if I told you that I *am* psychic?"

"I would say you're full of shit," he replies bluntly.

"Well, I'll just say this then, I went to college to

study American history, with an emphasis on Creole history, here in Louisiana. I'm from the area, and I love the folklore here. Most everything I tell you on this tour can be verified in history books."

"Only *most*?" he asks.

"Well, the rest of it depends on whether you believe in the paranormal or not, doesn't it? No one can *prove* the existence of ghosts. Even spirits caught on film can usually be explained away. Double-exposure, reflections, weird lighting, that sort of thing. And, yes, people have their own experiences, but that's just hearsay, right?"

"Do *you* believe in ghosts?" he asks me.

"Sugar, you can't live in New Orleans and *not* believe in ghosts. They're all over the place. So, yes, I do believe they exist."

"So, you're saying spirits are just roaming around, trying to dick with all of us?"

"No, not at all. In fact, not all ghosts are intelligent."

He blinks at me blankly.

"There are theories that some spirits are caught in a loop. Like...an echo. They do the same things over and over again, whether someone is there to see it or not. They don't know that anyone is there. They may not even know they're dead. It's like a recording.

"And then there are spirits that do know they're dead, and they haunt. Maybe they haunt a place or a thing or a person."

"Whoa." He holds up a hand and stops walking. "A person?"

"Sure, it's happened. For whatever reason, a spirit attaches itself to a living person, and no matter where the person moves or where they go, the spirit goes with them."

"Creepy AF," he says and grins at his friend, who's been standing by, listening silently.

"Now it's time to talk about more dead people," I say and wink as I stop in front of the LaLaurie mansion and reinforce my shields. Even though things have been routine on tonight's tour, this is the one place that still makes me uneasy.

Maybe because the woman who owned it—and still haunts it—was as evil as the man we just caught.

Maybe more so.

I'm only about thirty seconds into my speech about the mansion and its history when there is a loud pop and sparks fly everywhere from above.

We all duck out of the way and look around in confusion. Are we being shot at? Did a bomb just go off somewhere?

"The streetlight exploded!" someone exclaims, pointing to the light directly above me. I look up and, sure enough, smoke streams from where the bulb once was, and the filaments are still glowing from the explosion.

That's new.

At least there's no shadow hovering over it.

"Wow, is everyone okay?" I ask the group, looking everyone over. "Did anyone get hurt?"

"Just scared us," someone said.

"If that's part of the show, it's effective," someone shouts, making me laugh.

"No, that's definitely not part of the show. That was a freebie, just for you guys. Okay, well, now that your heart rate is up, let's talk about Madame LaLaurie..."

CHAPTER TWENTY-ONE

"Death always went with the territory."

-Richard Ramirez, The Night Stalker

Just look at her down there, he thinks to himself as he floats above the streetlamp that he successfully blew up. She's laughing and wandering through their city with her little group of idiots, who all want to know about the paranormal things that plague the French Quarter.

He always understood that Brielle needed to make a living, and that sharing her gifts with others was an efficient way for her to do so.

She does the best she can.

But she's capable of so much more.

He didn't realize that it would take him a while to figure out his new way of life. That he wouldn't slip easily between his physical body to the spiritual one and carry on the way he was before.

It seems there's a learning curve.

That displeases him. He's been following Brielle all week, trying to communicate with her, but she can't see him. Or, if she can, she's ignoring him. That's something he'll have to punish her for later.

But he's chosen to trust that it's not Brielle's fault. He simply has to work harder. Which is fine. Hard work has always come easily to him. He enjoys it.

He floats above the group as Brielle leads them through town. From his vantage point, he can see the other spirits she talks about, trapped in their own after-lives of torment.

He doesn't pity them. They earned what they got and where they are.

Just as he did.

But he's not trapped, he controls his destiny. And as soon as he figures out some things, he'll be right back on track.

He watches as Brielle smiles and says goodbye to a customer. She's so beautiful, his sweet girl.

Don't you worry, he thinks. *You haven't lost me, Brielle. I can't wait to show you what I have in store. You're going to be so happy. So excited. It won't be long now.*

CHAPTER TWENTY-TWO

Cash

"It's been a week," I say to Asher as I sit across from him in his office. I just arrived, and I want some answers.

And a conversation with a colleague.

Something's eating at me.

"How is Brielle?" Asher asks.

"She's doing well, actually." I rub the back of my neck and sigh. "She's gone back to work and says nothing strange has happened. The spirits of the girls are gone. Millie and Daphne have gone home. Everything seems to be back to normal."

"And you don't trust it," he guesses correctly.

"It's ridiculous, but you're right. I don't trust it. Catching him or discovering who he was wasn't an easy task, as you know. But then it was over and wrapped up so quickly it just seems...unfinished to me. Please tell me you found his body."

"We did," Asher confirms, and I feel my stomach loosen for the first time in a month. "He crawled into a ruined shed about a quarter-mile from his house. He bled out there. We're still waiting for an autopsy, but there was a huge amount of blood. As Sarah said, he was stabbed in the stomach."

"I'm surprised he made it a quarter of a mile. I wonder why he went that way instead of calling for help?"

"You know why. There's no way he could have called 911. He would have been caught."

"In which direction was the shed?" I ask. Asher reaches for a map, unrolls it on his desk, and we lean over it.

"Here's his house," Asher says and points to a red dot. "This is where we found him."

"I think this is Brielle's mother's house," I say, pointing to a property less than a mile away from the shed. "I wonder if he was headed there for help."

"Could be," Asher says. "My men stopped by there and tried to ask questions."

I lean back in the chair. "I bet that went well."

"She's crazy, Cash."

"I'm a licensed psychiatrist, and I can confirm that statement. She also killed her husband roughly twenty years ago."

The other man's eyes narrow. "Come again?"

"You heard me." I stand and pace the office. "I don't have proof, just the word of a crazy old woman and my girlfriend, who was only a teenager at the time."

"The house needs to be condemned. She needs to go to a mental hospital."

"I know." I turn to look at him.

"I'm reporting it to the proper authorities."

"Understood."

"Now, I have a whole slew of things to talk to you about regarding this case. I hope you don't have any plans for a few hours."

"I'm all ears," I reply as I return to my seat. "I have plenty to say, as well, but I'm anxious to hear what your team found in the house."

"More creepy shit than I like to think about," he says, shaking his head. Asher looks bone-tired. "He kept meticulous journals, dating back to when he was young. And he stored them in chronological order."

"That was thoughtful of him."

"Everything in that house was spotless. Tidy. Precise."

"Makes sense."

"Does it?"

"Oh, absolutely. He thrived on control, and that included his home. Everything had a place. He was clearly a planner. The girls he took may have been random in the heat of the moment, but he knew *when* he would take them, and he had a very particular type. He planned what he would do to them. Most likely, he practiced the same techniques for many years."

"You're right," Asher confirms. "He was fifty-four years old when he died. The first journal dates back to when he was sixteen. That's almost forty years of killing."

"Surely, he didn't start with humans."

"Animals," Asher says. "The family dog. A neighbor's cat. It escalated from there. He documented names if he knew them, so we have lists of his victims. Many families will have answers to the disappearances of their loved ones because of this."

"That's something, I guess. What else?"

"My team has spent the better part of this past week poring through every journal. They took notes on what they read. We counted one hundred and seventy-four victims, starting with his mother when he was eighteen."

"Christ Jesus."

"Those are just the human victims. We didn't count the animals, but there were a lot of those, as well. And, Cash, he wasn't just after Brielle."

"I saw the shrines for her sisters. He was going after them, too."

"He'd already started." Asher fishes out some photos and slaps them on the desk for me to see. "The eyeballs we found in that box? He said in a journal that he was collecting those for Daphne. Because she has the *sight*."

"There were almost a hundred eyes in that box. They're with the ME to determine if they're from ninety-six different victims, or if he took both eyes from each victim."

"He most likely took both," I say and move to the next photo. "Is this blood?"

"Thirty pints of it," Asher confirms. "It said in his notes that he was collecting it for Millie, because she's a kitchen witch, and he thought she could use it for potions."

"For fuck's sake, what kind of potions could she make with human blood?"

"I don't even want to guess," Asher says, sighing loudly. "He took the hair for Brielle, simply because he had a thing for her brunette hair. In his notes, he says that he didn't think he could take anything to help her gift of seeing shadows, but he could make sure no other women had hair nice enough to rival hers."

"Sick fuck," I whisper.

"So, he had trophies for each of the girls. The blood and eyes, he said, were the *practice* toys he'd played with to get ready for the main show. But he'd mastered his craft for Brielle and was nearing the end of the show. He'd planned to take her next week."

My head whips up in surprise. "He had it *planned*?"

"That shouldn't surprise you."

I shake my head and try to detach from Brielle, remove myself as her lover, and think of this from a professional standpoint.

"You're right. It shouldn't. And now that I think

about it, it doesn't surprise me. What was the last entry in the journal?"

"Here."

He flips to the last page of the journal and passes it to me.

April 23,

She came to me. Finally! I've heard her in the room of fun, talking to the girls, and hoped that she'd come to me, and she finally did. She saw everything. I've kept the house spotless in hopes that she'd arrive soon. She seemed very pleased and didn't even mind when I touched her. I don't think it occurred to her that I could touch her during her dream-walking.

Brielle and the others always underestimated me. They didn't know that I understood their gifts. That I share them. I could teach them so much! And I will, very soon.

Just a few more days, and Brielle will be here. In our home. I have to finish playing with the other toys first, but that won't take long. I have a couple more experiments to run on them before I feel comfortable using the techniques on my Brielle. I want to give her the best experience of her life. I want to provide her with things that no one else ever has.

It's going to be so beautiful!

I toss the book on the desk and swallow hard.

"When will the autopsy be done?"

"Sometime this week," Asher says. "The morgue's been a little busy the past few weeks."

"Yeah. What happens to him when it's done?"

"Well, this is where it gets weird."

"*This* is where it gets weird?"

He pulls out another document and passes it to me. "That's his will. He left everything to Brielle and her sisters."

My eyes scan it. "He had it done through an attorney and everything."

"He wasn't a stupid man. An evil one, but not stupid."

"So now they own the property and all of his personal effects."

"Yes, and as next of kin, they get to decide what to do with his remains."

"Well, that's pretty fucked-up, Asher."

"Oh, trust me. This is the weirdest case of my career, and like I told you before, I've seen some shit. This rivals some of the most extreme serial killer cases I've heard of."

"Same here, and I've also seen some shit. But there's something that I can't put my finger on that tells me this isn't entirely over."

"He's on ice in the morgue," Asher reminds me. "It's pretty much over."

"Yeah." I stare at all of the evidence on Asher's desk. "Yeah, I guess you're right. How in the hell am I going to tell the girls that the sick fuck who wanted them all tortured and dead left all of his worldly possessions to them?"

"I can tell them," Asher offers.

"No, it should come from me." I sigh again and

stand. "How soon do you need to know what they want to do with his remains?"

"No rush at all."

"Good. I'll be in touch."

I'm on my way out of the police station when my phone rings.

"Hey, Felicia. How's it going over there?"

"Well, we're at the ER," Felicia says. I can tell she's trying to sound like nothing's wrong, but something's wrong. "I didn't want to worry you, but I thought you should know."

"What's up?"

"I just didn't like the sound of your mom's breathing. She says it's nothing, that she always wheezes like that, but she didn't sound this way when I arrived. So, I brought her in just to get checked out."

"Good idea. Please keep me posted. I need to call Andy. I haven't talked to him in a few days."

"You've been a little busy," she replies kindly. "But he'd like to hear from you. I think he's getting a little lonely without me."

"I'll get in touch with him today. Thanks, Felicia."

"You're welcome. Talk soon."

Before I can put my phone into my pocket, my brother calls.

"Did you just talk to my wife?" he asks after I answer.

"Just hung up with her."

"I'm worried about Mom. The last time she had pneumonia, she almost died."

"We don't know that she has pneumonia. She could have allergies."

"Yeah." I can hear the strain in my brother's voice. "You're right."

"Why don't I come by and take you out to lunch? Are you free?"

"I have some time."

"I'm still at the police station. I'm sitting on the steps out front."

"Be right there."

He hangs up, and I shoot Brielle a text.

Me: *Hey, babe. Gonna grab lunch with Andy. Need anything?*

I grin when I see the dots bounce as she replies.

Brielle: *Have fun! I don't need anything. I'm at Daphne's store, having lunch with the sisters.*

Me: *I'll text when I'm done.*

I've never been to Daphne's store. We always meet at either Brielle's apartment or Witches Brew, but Brielle told me that Daphne owns an antique shop.

I bet there are a lot of antiques in New Orleans.

"I didn't know you were still working on the case," Andy says as he approaches.

I stand and join him on the sidewalk. "Yeah, there are still things to tie up. That man was on a level of evil I've never seen before."

"I'm glad you were here to help with it," Andy says.

"I don't know how you do what you do. I think it would drive me insane."

"I put the cases in boxes," I say as we walk into a restaurant nearby. We're quickly shown to a table. "I have to compartmentalize it all. Because you're right, it messes with you. The last case, losing Carlson—"

"Which was *not* your fault."

"That one got under my skin. And, frankly, you wouldn't be human if they didn't get under your skin a little bit. But you have to put it all in boxes, or it will consume you.

"I don't know how I'm going to make a relationship with Brielle work."

"Why?"

"Because what I do takes me all over the damn world, Andy. I haven't seen the inside of my apartment in Dallas for at least two months. I don't even know why I have it. Not to mention, you said yourself that I see some horrible shit. That'll bleed into any relationship."

"First, I want to know how *this* case has affected you."

"It messed with me," I admit, knowing I can trust my brother. "Because it was less black and white than any other case I've worked. I've never had to deal with the paranormal. I didn't think I believed in it before."

"And now?" We pause as the waitress approaches and takes our orders.

"I've seen it," I say bluntly when she leaves. "At first,

I humored Brielle. *She* believed it, so I just went along with it. But what she described, and what she's able to do? That's not a hoax, man. And it's not anything I can explain, even with all of my years of education and training. It just *is*. So, yeah, I believe it. Not to mention, I saw a friggin' ghost myself, so..."

"Whose ghost?"

"The killer's. He was standing in the middle of the goddamn road, I shit you not."

"Whoa." Andy sits back in his chair, his eyes wide and pinned to mine. "You're kidding."

"I wish I was."

"And how do you feel about Brielle?"

"I'm completely and irrevocably in love with her."

A slow smile spreads over my brother's face. "It finally happened."

"Not sure what I can do about it, though," I repeat. "My job doesn't lend itself well to marriage."

"I didn't say anything about *marriage*."

I laugh and shrug. "Yeah, well, that's usually what happens when you decide you can't live without someone, right? She's it for me, and I don't know how to make it work."

"I know the NOPD would hire you in a heartbeat. Not to mention, there's an FBI field office right here. You can transfer. You have options."

"I most likely wouldn't be a profiler anymore, though, and I worked my ass off to get here. You know that."

"Profiler, or be with the love of your life?" He holds up his hands at his sides as if he's weighing something on scales. "I mean, I think it's a no-brainer, man."

"I know." I sigh. "Now, let's get back to you. How are you doing?"

"I miss my wife," he says with a frown. "She needs to get home."

"We're just a couple of lovesick fools."

"Ain't it great?"

I'M glad I had lunch with my brother. He always gives me a different perspective on things, and I feel better after talking with him.

He's not wrong.

If I move here permanently, not only would I have Brielle, but I'd also have Andy and Felicia.

It's damn tempting.

More than tempting.

Let's be honest, it's probably going to happen.

I push through the door of Reflections, Daphne's store on the edge of the French Quarter, and smile when I see all three sisters sitting in a corner, drinking coffee.

"There he is," Brielle says with a grin and leaps up to offer me a kiss. "I missed you today."

"Same here." I lay another deep kiss on her before we join the others. "I love your place here, Daph."

The pretty redhead grins and glances around her store. "Me, too. I could sure tell you some interesting stories here, Cash."

"Yeah? Like what?"

She stands and places her hand on a tall, yellow vase. "This was made in 1923 by a man who lived in the bayou. He made it for his wife, who was about to have their first baby. Yellow was Mildred's favorite color, and he had to do something to keep his hands busy while they waited on the child. He was so excited."

Daphne's face turns sad.

"But when Mildred went into labor, something went wrong. Both she and the baby died. So, he gave this vase to his cousin, who lived here in New Orleans."

"That's horrible," Millie whispers.

"You can do that with every piece in here?" I ask.

She nods and sits in the chair again. "I can do that with literally *everything*. I see the thoughts of the people who sat in airplane seats before me. I see pretty much everything, Cash."

"That has to be exhausting."

"I'm able to block a lot of it because I've learned to build my shields of protection, and Millie makes me potions for strength. It takes a lot to surprise me these days."

I turn to Millie. "And you're proficient in potions and spells and such?"

"Yes, I'm a hedgewitch," she confirms. "I've studied for years. I'm also psychic, but not in the same way these two are. I don't see the past or dead people. I read people's minds. I can touch someone and see their thoughts, feelings, things like that. So, I try to avoid skin-on-skin contact most of the time unless I take precautions."

"Fascinating," I mutter. "You're all remarkable and more interesting than I can say."

"I like your boyfriend, Bri," Daphne says, grinning. "He hands out compliments. He can stay."

"I'm glad you approve," Brielle says with a laugh. "Now, tell us what you found out today."

"You're not going to like it."

CHAPTER TWENTY-THREE

Brielle

"What's going on?" I ask Cash. I don't like the concern in his green eyes at all.

"First of all, they found his body," he says, and all three of us slump in relief. "He was in an old shed between his house and your mother's."

"He must have been trying to get to Mama, to see if she could help him," Millie says.

"As a sidebar," Cash continues, "speaking of your mother, the police visited her house while they were canvassing the area, looking for his body. They're going to recommend she be institutionalized, and the house condemned."

I blink at him, then look at my sisters. "It's for the best."

"Then why does it feel...*not* for the best?" Daphne asks.

"Maybe they can help her," Millie says. "Maybe

getting out of that haunted house and being among professionals who can treat her will help. It won't make her a nice person, but it has to be better than how she's living now."

"Agreed," I say and nod. "So far, this isn't awful."

"Yeah, well, buckle up," Cash mutters. "I spoke at length with Asher today. They've been gathering all of the evidence from his residence, cataloging and poring through it all. His team has worked very hard on this."

"Of course, they have," I agree.

"Horace was an intelligent man. Do you mind if I pace, Daphne?"

"Of course not, pace away, just keep talking."

Cash stands and walks back and forth, speaking as he thinks. "He kept journals. From day one."

"How long?" Millie asks.

"Nearly forty years," Cash responds. "I'm going to be brutally honest with you all because you deserve to know the truth, but it's not comforting information."

"We need to know," I say firmly. "And after what we've all recently gone through, I think we can take it."

"Agreed," Daphne says, as Millie nods enthusiastically. "Just tell us everything."

Cash swallows hard and then starts to tell us about the journals. The eyes, the blood, and the hair. Horace's past and plans for the future come rushing out of him in a tidal wave, leaving us all breathless and wide-eyed.

"He eventually wanted *all* of you," Cash says at the end. "And he was moving down the line, one at a time.

But for years, he practiced, honing his skills, perfecting his plans."

"Why us?" I wonder aloud. "I mean, it's not like we knew him that well. He was just some guy that lived nearby and used to help our parents from time to time. Sure, he may have been sleeping with our mother, but it's not like we spent holidays with the man or called him *Uncle Horace* or anything."

"Well, I have theories on that," Millie says, surprising me. "I remember when I was young, like maybe ten, Mama told me that I was Horace's daughter."

Daphne and I gasp in horror.

"Don't freak," Millie says, holding up a hand. "She was lying. Mama *always* lied. She thought it was fun to dick with people's minds, remember? I'm absolutely *not* related to that man in any way. But I wonder if she told Horace the same thing, and he believed her?"

"What if she told him that we're all his children?" Daphne asks.

"And so he wanted to kill his supposed daughters?" I ask. "That doesn't make sense."

"Serial killers aren't rational," Cash reminds me. "Just because they're smart, it doesn't make them sane. So, if what Millie says is true, it's absolutely possible that he believed you were his kids, and that's where the fixation came from. We can only speculate on why he turned to sexually sadistic torture and murder versus requesting a simple DNA test."

"Well, that's some messed-up shit," Millie says with a sigh. "Not that it wasn't already. Thanks for telling us."

"I'm not done," Cash says. "There's more."

"*More?*" I ask.

"Oh, yeah. This is where it gets bad."

"*This* is where it gets bad?" Daphne says, letting out a half-laugh. "Great. Give it to us."

"The three of you are his next of kin."

We sit silently, watching as Cash stops pacing and turns to the three of us.

"Did you hear me?" he asks again.

"So you *know* that he's our father? Pretty sure that was a horrible joke," Millie says.

"I wish it were," he replies gently. "And I don't know about the DNA, but Horace had a very detailed will. It's legal, and he names the three of you as equal beneficiaries, inheriting all of his property."

"Burn it," I announce angrily. "Burn it all to the fucking ground."

"Great idea," Daphne says.

"And that means," Cash continues, "that as executors of the estate, you have to decide what to do with his remains."

"Burn them with the fucking house," I reply.

"I'm quite sure you can do that," Cash says with a nod. "Though maybe not *with* the house." He grins. "No decision needs to be made at this time. The house is still a crime scene, and no autopsy has been done yet, so there's no need to make a decision today."

"I say burn it all," I repeat and stare at the teacup I have resting in my lap. I scowl as, right before my eyes, the warm liquid splashes over the rim and onto my leg. "Hey! What the hell?"

"Did you spill?" Daphne asks.

"No. I was just sitting here, and it just...sloshed over the side."

"By itself?" Millie asks.

"Yes. By itself."

"You're upset," Cash says reasonably, and I turn my scowl on him.

"I'm not an idiot. I'm telling you, I didn't spill it."

"Okay." He holds up his hands in surrender. "I believe you."

"I don't know what to believe anymore," Daphne admits with a sigh. "Everything is just so...odd."

"Well, at least the worst of it is over," Millie says.

"Don't jinx it," I reply.

***

"CASH?" I wander through my apartment later that night, after I return home from work.

"Back here," he says. I find him in the guest room, where he's set up a makeshift office. "How are you?"

"Tired," I admit, a small smile forming as I climb onto his lap and nuzzle his neck. I love how strong his arms feel wrapped around me. "I'm sorry I snapped at you earlier today."

"I'd snap at me, too," he says and kisses my hair. "It's been a lot."

"A lot of what?" I raise my head so I can look him in the eyes. I absolutely love his green eyes.

"Just a lot," he says, leaning in to kiss my lips lightly. "And I haven't really asked you how you're holding up."

"I'm actually doing pretty well, all things considered." And it's true. I feel good. I feel relieved more than anything. "I guess today's news threw me for a loop."

"Me, too."

"I thought we were done with all of it, and then to find out that we're not, it's just like he continues taunting us even though he's long gone, you know?"

"I know. It's not fair."

"Can we refuse to be the next of kin?"

"I don't know the laws and regulations surrounding that," he says as he brushes his fingers through my hair. "I suppose you could, but then I imagine the estate would go to the state, and God only knows what they'll do with it."

"True." I nibble my lip, enjoying the way his fingers feel in my hair. "I guess we'll end up doing something about it."

"You don't have to think about it today," he reminds me. "So, set it aside for now. There's no need to worry."

"You're right."

He frames my face, his long fingers cupping my chin

as he lays his lips over mine, consuming me with passion and lust.

There's always so much lust where Cash is concerned.

Suddenly, I pull back and stare at him in horror.

"What is it?"

"Your hands are on my face."

"Yes?"

"Who the hell is brushing my hair?"

It stops. I scratch my scalp and shiver.

"What do you mean, Brielle?"

"Someone was brushing their fingers through my hair. I thought it was you."

"No, I was holding you, and then I was kissing the hell out of you."

I stare at him, then stand and shake my hair out. "Do I have bugs in my hair?"

"Not that I can see." He joins me, and it's his hands brushing through my hair now. "No, I don't see anything at all."

"That's so creepy." I shiver again. "I mean, I know I have spirits in this apartment, but they've *never* touched me before."

"Have spirits *ever* touched you?"

"No, I just see them," I reply. "And it's all back to shadows now, which is a relief."

I move to clutch my stone pendant, but it's not around my neck.

"What's wrong?" Cash asks.

"I keep losing my damn necklace." I walk over to my bedroom and sigh when I see it lying on my pillow. "I don't know how it got here, but at least it's here. I'll put it on later."

"Look, I think you've had a lot on your mind," Cash says, wrapping his arms around me from behind. "I suggest you take a long, hot shower, have some tea, and then I'm going to make love to you for the rest of the night."

"The *whole* night?"

"Do you think I can't do that?"

"I mean, that's a pretty bold offer, but I'll take it." I spin in his arms and grin as he kisses me deeply, those amazing hands cupping my ass and pulling me against the length of him. I can feel his already firm cock against my belly. "Maybe we should do some sex stuff before my shower."

"I can wait." He kisses my nose. "Come on."

He leads me into the bathroom, where he proceeds to turn on the water and adjust the temperature. He helps me out of my clothes and holds my hand as I step over the side of the tub into the hot spray of the shower.

"Okay, you were right. This is nice."

"I love it when I'm right," he says, making me grin.

"Why don't you come in here and wash my back?"

"If I come in there, darlin', you won't get clean." He pokes his head around the shower curtain. "Take your time. I'll brew you some tea."

"You're handy to have around," I call after him and listen to him chuckle as he walks out of the bathroom.

I do enjoy having Cash around, and it's not just for his tea-making skills or even the intense sex we have almost every day. It's so much deeper than any of that.

There are times that I feel like he's an extension of me, and vice versa. We haven't talked about what will happen once his vacation time is over, and he has to go back to his life from before.

I don't want to think about the possibility that he'll leave, and that this will just be a fond, sexy memory mixed in with the scariest time of my life.

We've shared so much together over the past month. How in the world will I ever go back to being without him, as if he were never here?

I turn and get my hair wet, then reach for the shampoo, thinking it over.

I suppose I could ask Millie to make me a potion to forget he ever existed. But that seems even sadder than the thought of not seeing him anymore. At least, this way, I'll have the memories of us, even if they make my heart hurt.

I don't want him to go.

But I can't go with him.

And I can't make him stay if that's not what he wants.

I don't have any additional answers once my hair is rinsed of both shampoo and conditioner. One thing I do know is that he's here now, and I'm going to enjoy every moment I have with him, no matter what.

I push back the curtain and reach for a towel to wipe my face and wrap it around my wet hair. Then I grab a second towel to dry my body as I step out of the shower. I wrap the terrycloth around me and frown when I see my necklace sitting on the lip of the sink.

It was on my pillow. I left it there earlier. I know I did.

Cash must have brought it in for me. He's so thoughtful. I reach for it and pull the long chain over my head, then see movement on the fog-covered mirror.

A chill runs down my spine.

An invisible finger is marking up the fog on the glass.

I'm still here. H.

I back up and reach for the doorknob.

"What's wrong?"

I hear Cash in the other room, and there's pounding on the door now, but I can't get the knob to turn.

"Brielle, what's wrong in there?"

"I can't open the door!"

"Let go of it."

I do as he asks and glance back to see the writing still there. Cash gets the door open and rushes in.

"Why did you scream?"

"I screamed?"

"A blood-curdling one."

I simply point to the mirror. "He's still here, Cash."

"He wrote that?"

I don't have time to speak before another word is written on the glass.

Yes.

CHAPTER TWENTY-FOUR

"I can't stand a bitchy chick."

-Gerald Stano

Burn it all down?

If he could hit her, Brielle would be lying in her own blood right now.

The rage is all-encompassing but stronger than it ever was when he was still alive. The emotions in the afterlife are intense.

Brielle, one of only three people he's loved his whole life, just said that she'd like to burn down everything he worked for. And her sisters didn't stand up for him. They didn't even bat an eye!

How could they? How *dare* they? Don't they know how hard he worked, day in and day out, to make something beautiful for them? It's clear they're nothing but three entitled, spoiled, horrible girls. He needs to teach them a lesson.

He won't be making anything wonderful for them anymore. No, that time has passed. They've ruined that with their ugliness.

Instead, he's going to punish them in ways they never imagined. The ways he killed his toys will pale in comparison to what he has planned for his daughters.

He didn't raise them to be this way, did he?

If Ruth had given him the chance to discipline them more, maybe things would be different. Perhaps he would have had an opportunity to make it good for his girls.

But, no. She taunted him with them. Though that's what women do, isn't it? They tease, and they condemn, and they open their legs to get satisfied, and then they flick you off like an annoying fly.

Ruth.

Maybe he should make a trip to her house to punish her, as well. She deserves it.

They all do.

He wandered away from the girls after Brielle talked about burning his things. Not just his things, *their* things. Everything he did, he did for them.

But now that it's theirs, they don't want it.

He was so blinded by rage, he was able to spill the tea, but that wasn't nearly satisfying enough.

He wishes he were at full strength so he could take care of matters correctly.

But he's getting there.

He spilled the tea.

He moved the necklace several times.

And, tonight, he ran his fingers through Brielle's glorious hair. It calmed him for a moment until she started speaking about him again.

He was wrong.

She doesn't love him.

And now she's in the shower. He can see her naked body, the way the water runs over her breasts and her tight nipples. She washes herself—*down there*—and he feels himself harden, even though he no longer has a physical body.

How?

How can he get sexually excited after death?

It makes no sense.

Once she gets out of the shower, he sets the necklace on the sink and laughs when she spies it and frowns in confusion.

That's right, little girl. I'm playing with you.

She mumbles to herself.

He wants her attention so badly, needs to make her understand that he isn't gone.

He focuses on the mirror and, with a great deal of effort, writes a message on the glass.

He's even able to reply to a question.

But the effort is too much for him, it drains him, and he fades away.

He needs to regroup and grow stronger so he can use his power when he needs it the most.

CHAPTER TWENTY-FIVE

Cash

"I'll call Asher." I reach for my phone, but Brielle lays her hand on my arm, stopping me.

"I told you before, this isn't something you can kill with a gun. I'm afraid the police can't help us with this."

I've never felt so helpless in all my life. Even the Carlson case didn't frustrate me like this.

"What *can* help us, then?"

She bites her lip, fiddling with the stone around her neck. Finally, she moves past me and into her bedroom, where she simultaneously drops the towel and reaches for her phone.

"I have to call my sisters," she says, absently dialing a number and pressing her cell to her ear as she reaches for clothes to toss on. "He's still here. Yeah. I'll tell you all about it, but I'm scared, Mill. We have to figure out how to get rid of this bastard for good. Uh-huh. Okay."

She hangs up and tosses the phone on the bed.

"What did she say?"

"She's calling Miss Sophia, and then she'll call me back. I'm going to call Daphne in just a sec."

I quirk my brow as she launches herself into my arms and clings to me, her nose pressed to my chest.

"Hey, it's okay, darlin'."

"No, it's not." She tightens her grasp. "But it will be. And I have a feeling the next few days are going to get scarier, and maybe super weird. So, I want to take a second to say thank you. Thank you for not running away, and for being a rock in the middle of all this chaos."

"There's nowhere else I'd rather be." I kiss her hair, breathing her in. "We're going to get rid of this asshole, once and for all."

"You're right." She smiles up at me, just as her phone lights up. "I have to take that. But when this is all over, *again*, I want to curl up in bed with you for a few days without leaving it. I want to snuggle and watch bad movies and eat junk food."

"Can we be naked?"

"Sure," she says with a laugh.

"And why do they have to be *bad* movies? Let's watch good ones."

She laughs in earnest, holding her phone in her palm. "Deal. Good movies and nakedness. Any other requests?"

"As long as you're there with me, I'm good to go."

She winks at me as she answers the phone and

presses it to her ear. "Yes. Oh, that's so nice of her. Okay. Did you call Daph? Awesome, we'll meet you there in thirty. Thanks. Love you, too."

She hangs up and turns to me.

"Millie talked to Miss Sophia, and she wants all of us to come to her house right away. This is good news, Cash. She's powerful and knows *so much*. She can help."

"Are you sure you want me there?"

She grabs my hand and presses it to her face. "Yes. I want you with me."

"Let's do this."

The drive to Miss Sophia's takes longer than the drive to the women's mother's house. Miss Sophia lives even deeper in the bayou. Her cabin is warm, even from the outside and in the dark. Smoke billows from a chimney. Plants and flowers line the porch, hang in boxes under the windows, and cover every available surface.

It looks like something out of a fairy tale.

But Miss Sophia is the good witch, not the one that eats little children.

"Come in," the woman says from the doorway, ushering us in. "Your sisters are already here. I also called in some help."

I feel my eyes widen in surprise when we cross the threshold. The house doesn't look big enough from the outside to hold this many people.

I recognize Mallory. The rest are strangers to me.

"This is my granddaughter," Sophia says, gesturing

to a beautiful, blond woman sitting at an old, wooden dining room table. "Lena, this is—"

"Cash," Lena finishes for her with a smile.

"Are you psychic, too?"

"Absolutely," she says, her pretty smile widening. "But also, Mallory and Grandmama have told me about you. It's nice to meet you."

"Likewise."

I'm introduced to other men and women of different ages and races, and then I finally sit by Daphne and let out a sigh.

"It's a lot to take in," Daphne says with a nod.

"Am I sitting in the middle of a coven?"

Daphne grins. "Several, actually. Don't look so surprised. This is Louisiana. There are a lot of people here."

"And a lot of witches, apparently."

"That, too," she agrees. "Millie's over there with a woman named Harmony, still poring through our grandmother's book."

"Why is it taking so long?"

"Because a good chunk of it is written in languages we don't understand," Daphne explains. "But Harmony does, so she's helping Millie."

"Who's the guy on the opposite side of the table? He looks...angry."

"That's Lucien. He's not angry, he's brooding. He's a brilliant warlock. He's only thirty-five but has the wisdom of an old man who's been studying his whole life. Magic comes naturally to him, but then again, it should. His family has been in the lifestyle for hundreds of years."

"Interesting." I watch as Lucien glances up from the book in front of him and takes a couple of seconds to study Millie, and then, as if he catches himself, he looks back down at the pages on the table. "He has a thing for Millie."

"Oh, absolutely," Daphne agrees, nodding. "He's for her. She won't admit it, though."

"Why?"

"I don't know if you've noticed, but we tend to be stubborn women."

I chuckle and shrug a shoulder. "I will admit to no such thing."

"Smart man." She laughs as she watches her sister and Lucien. "They'll figure it out when the time is right."

"Now you sound like your sister."

"What a lovely compliment." She pats my arm. "I like you, Cash. And I like you even better for my sister. Speaking of which, I'd better see what she and Miss Sophia have cooking over there."

She stands and leaves me, and I watch her cross the room to Brielle and Miss Sophia. They're not just cooking up ideas, they're literally *cooking* in the kitchen.

I glance around the room again and realize that I don't have anything to offer these people in way of help. At least, not right now.

And I'm antsy.

And more than a little angry.

It's in my nature—and training—to investigate. So, that's what I'll do.

"Brielle," I say as I approach her. "I'm going to call Andy and see if he can go over the crime scene with me tonight."

"Tonight?" She turns and stares up at me as if I'm nuts. In fact, the whole room has gone quiet. "But it's almost midnight. It's *dark*."

"Andy will be with me," I remind her. "No one is there, Brielle. Aside from some wildlife, there's nothing there that can harm us."

"But, I—"

"Let him go," Miss Sophia says, watching me. "But please, take these. And ask your brother to drink his. It'll protect you both."

She passes me two bottles, cold from the fridge. I don't even ask what's in them.

I've learned to just do as asked without asking questions. And, most of the time, it's delicious anyway.

"Please be careful." Brielle clings to me. "Be very careful."

"We'll be back here before you know it." I kiss her hair. "I have to do something while y'all work. I have to *work*."

"I know." She smiles bravely. "It's fine. Everything's going to be fine."

"You'll be safe," Sophia assures us all. "Please return

here when you're done. And bring Andy with you. I'll cleanse you both."

Once again, I don't ask questions. "Yes, ma'am."

"WHAT IN THE hell are we doing out here in the dark?" Andy demands as we get out of our cars and meet at the porch. The light is on. The last investigators out here must have left it on.

"I want to do some digging," I reply simply. "And I didn't want to do it by myself."

"It's creepy as fuck out here," my brother grumbles as I slice through the police tape over the front entrance with my pocketknife and open the door. I flick on the lights inside.

"You've seen way creepier than this," I assure him as we slip inside, and I shut the door behind us.

"Uh, I don't think so. I don't spend much time in the bayou. Especially at night."

"So, the bastard's dead, but he's not *gone*."

"What does that mean?"

"It means his spirit is still dicking with my girl, and it's pissing me the hell off. Brielle and her sisters are currently with the rest of their witchy friends, trying to find an answer to the billion-dollar question of how to get him gone for good."

"And you decided to bring me out here."

"I wanted to look around, yes. Maybe there's something here the investigators missed."

"It looks like they took everything," Andy says, looking around the small cabin. He's right, it doesn't look anything like it did last week when we were here. Even the furniture is gone, most likely taken into evidence.

We walk the space, using the flashlights on our phones to light up the areas under the sinks, and in the cabinets.

"Damn it, my phone died," Andy says with a scowl. "I had a full battery when I got here."

"Odd," I murmur, checking my phone. I'm down to ten percent.

I also arrived with a full battery.

I turn the flashlight off to save power.

"Come on. This is the really fucked-up room." I lead Andy to the back of the house, where Horace used to hold the girls.

I flick on the lights.

"Jesus Christ," my brother breathes as he walks in behind me.

"They took the beds." I gesture to the wall opposite us. "There were three toddler-sized beds there where he tied them up. Over there was the workbench and all of his tools, and in that corner was an electric chair."

"The blood on the floor," he whispers. "Jesus, Cash, there must be *gallons*."

I nod, taking it all in. I don't know why we're here. I don't know what I expect to find. The police took *every-*

thing to test for blood and other bodily fluids, and to discover hairs...*anything*.

"The smell is still rank," I say as we pace the space. "I would think that after they took out the girls and all of his tools, the smell would lessen."

"It should," Andy agrees, then stops and sets his hands on his hips.

I walk toward him, and then he holds his hand up. "Stop."

"What?"

"Walk that path again."

I do as he asks, and when I turn around, I see him eyeing the floor.

"Do it again."

I walk back and forth several times.

"What do you see?"

"It's not what I see, it's what I hear. I think there's something under us."

The hair stands up on the back of my neck. "You're kidding."

"No, I'm not."

We walk to the door that leads out of the room then out to a tall deck that hovers over the swamp.

"It's water," I point out when I turn on my flashlight and shine it on the swamp below. "No door to a basement. I don't think there could *be* a basement."

"I'm telling you, it sounded hollow in one spot when you walked over it."

"This is an old house," I remind him as we go back

inside. "It's bound to sound weird. Make odd noises."

He shakes his head and walks back and forth. He's pushing against one board with his toe when, suddenly, the board pops up as if it's loose.

"Bingo," Andy says triumphantly.

We pry the board out and reveal a trap door. It fits so seamlessly into the floor of the room that there's no way anyone would know it's there unless they *put* it there.

"Do you have enough battery in your phone for this?" Andy asks me.

"I hope so, because I'm not going down there in the dark," I reply, just before we pull up the door, revealing a ladder that descends into a deep, wide room.

"There's a switch." He flips it, and lights come on below. "Cash."

"I see it."

"My God."

We're both lying on our stomachs, staring into the room below.

"It has to be lined with iron or something strong that keeps the water out," I murmur. "And I'd love to know how he got all of those freezers down there."

"Dozens of them," Andy says then looks up at me. "You get *zero* guesses as to what's in them."

"Looks like we're going down."

I put my phone in my pocket and head down first. The ladder is sturdy, not creaking in the least as we make our descent.

The freezers run along the perimeter of the room, side by side, on all four walls.

I haven't even thought about what could possibly be in the cupboards above the freezers.

Once Andy's beside me, I flex my hand and then reach out for a handle.

"You've got to be kidding me."

Bodies? Yes, but cut up into parts in this one. It looks like this is a freezer full of hands. The next one is legs. And then heads.

Dozens of heads, staring forward but missing their eyes.

In one massive chest freezer, we find three intact stacked bodies.

"Cupboards," Andy says with a grim sigh. "The smell is worse."

"You open it."

He shakes his head but does as I ask.

Jars of hearts. At least, that's what they look like. One cupboard has nothing but intestines.

Not in jars.

Another cabinet has rows and rows of containers of blood.

"It looks like when someone's mom cans tomatoes to get through the winter," Andy says. "Blood-style. Was he a fucking vampire?"

"No, he was collecting the blood for Millie. At least, that's what he said in his diary."

"Sick fuck."

I open another cabinet, but there are no body parts. There's nothing but a huge, black book.

I take it off the shelf and pass it to Andy.

"Don't open that. I don't know what's in it, or if it's spelled. I'm going to take it back to Brielle and Miss Sophia. Maybe it's something they can use."

"I wouldn't know what to do with it even if I did open it," he says with a laugh.

"I have to call Asher and get the teams out here again. Tonight."

I pull my phone out of my pocket to call, but it's dead.

"Son of a bitch."

"Why did our phones die?" Andy asks.

"Well, some people say that ghosts can suck the battery life out of electronics," I reply and shrug.

"Are you saying this place is haunted?"

I look at him like he's crazy, and then glance around this room of horrors. "Look around you, brother. More people have died in this house than maybe in any other in the world, aside from perhaps a hospital. I'd be shocked if it's *not* haunted."

"Yeah. You're right. Let's go up so you can plug it in and call. You'll have a better signal anyway."

I nod, but as we move toward the ladder, the lights go out.

The door slams shut.

"What the fuck?"

I try to turn on my phone, but it stays black.

"Shit. My phone died, remember?"

"Are you telling me we're stuck down here in the dark with no cell?"

"I don't know that we're stuck."

I fumble in the dark until I find the ladder, then climb it. I find the switch, and when I flip it up, the lights come back on.

"Ghosts fucking with us."

"Let's get the hell out of here."

"Get that out of my house," Miss Sophia says, pointing at Andy. "That grimoire will not stay."

"I'm sorry," I say immediately, and Andy takes the book back to his car. "We found it at the house and thought it might be something you could use."

"I know your intentions were good, but that thing is pure evil."

Andy returns and apologizes.

"Come in, both of you," Sophia says, calmer now. "It's time you learn more about Horace."

We join the others, sitting at the table.

"We've spent the past few hours reading and studying everything available to us," Sophia begins. "And we know how to defeat him, but it won't be easy.

"Horace is the son of Babette Jarreau. The Jarreau family has been immersed in magic for hundreds of years, perhaps longer than your family, Lucien. All of our families were friends of theirs, and all was fine. Until Babette."

"I've heard stories," Lucien agrees, standing. "Do you mind?"

"By all means. I suspect you may know more about this."

Lucien nods. "My great-grandmother, Adelaide, was Babette's grandmother's sister," he says. "It's said that Babette was born with evil inside her. She gravitated to the black arts, insisted that they practice on the dark side, despite the teachings and beliefs of her family. She was banished from her coven and from her family, and she seemed to be fine with that.

"I don't know who fathered Horace. Babette was a mean, strict mother, who manipulated her son to do her bidding. She was also a jealous woman because Horace had more skill when it came to the craft. But all she gave him was black magic. Never the benevolent kind. That's all I know, or at least what's been told to me."

"As far as I can see, it's the truth," Sophia says with a nod. "And that book you found substantiates the tales. That book carries evil within it."

"Can't say I love the idea of it being in my car," Andy says, shaking his head.

"We will cleanse you and the vehicle," Sophia assures him. "But first, you have a phone call to make, yes?"

"Yes. Our phones died. Brielle, can I please borrow yours?"

"Of course."

CHAPTER TWENTY-SIX

Brielle

"Was your phone low when you got there?" I ask him, trying to keep the urgency out of my voice. The answer to this question is vital.

"No," he says flatly. "We both had full charges. Both phones died within fifteen minutes of being there."

I glance at Millie, who slowly shakes her head back and forth.

That means there's a ghost, or ghost*s*, sucking the electrical charge out of any equipment on site.

It means the place is haunted.

I don't know how many spirits we may be talking about.

Cash speaks into the phone, and I notice the whole room goes quiet once again, everybody listening.

"Dozens," Cash says and finds my eyes with his bright green ones. "It's a room under the torture room. There are freezers filled with bodies, cupboards filled with organs and blood. The team needs to be out there now, gathering everything. I don't know. Yes, I can meet you there."

"No," I say immediately and reach for his hand. "I don't want you to go back."

"I'll see you soon," he says into the phone and then hangs up and passes it back to me.

"It's not safe there."

"Brielle, I'm part of the investigation, and trust me when I tell you, what we found needs to be catalogued and taken *tonight*."

"I'm not disagreeing. Wait...*dozens*?"

"More than that," Andy confirms, his face grim. "He's been hunting for a long time, Brielle."

"I assumed he was just throwing all of the bodies into the swamp," Cash adds. "That would make sense. But he wasn't. He stored many of them right there in the house."

I cover my mouth with my hands, staring at Cash in horror. "Oh, my goddess."

"We're going to put a stop to all of this," Sophia assures us all. "But we have to work together. He's too strong for the three sisters to do it alone, and the six aren't ready."

"What six?" Cash asks.

"Not ready," Sophia repeats, putting an end to the discussion.

"We have to burn it all," I say to Cash. "The house, the body, that book. Everything. Under the full moon."

"And when is the full moon?" Cash asks.

"Tomorrow night."

"Handy," Andy says with a grin. "We can just get it all done and over with."

"Even more reason for me to get over there and meet Asher so those bodies can be taken out and given proper burials."

"He's right," Sophia says. "He's safe from the evil there. We've made it so. And we have plenty of work to do to get ready for tomorrow night."

I nod, take Cash's hand in mine, and lead him out the door and to his car.

"I need you to wear this." I take off my necklace and loop it over his head. "Don't take it off. It'll protect you."

"You need it," he says.

"Not here, I don't. I'm safer here than anywhere else in the world. You take it. Promise me you won't take it off."

"I promise." He leans in and presses his lips gently to mine. "Are you okay, sweetheart?"

"No. I'm scared, and I'm worried. As long as you stay safe, I'll be okay."

"That's my line," he says against my lips. "Just keep thinking about that day in bed. I'm going to cash in on that very soon."

"See that you do."

I love you.

I want to tell him now more than ever. So, I lean

close and press my lips to his ear.

"I love you more than anything, Cassien Winslow. Please stay safe tonight."

I could feel he was about to pull away, but instead, he tugs me hard against him, crushing me in a hug. "You can't get rid of me so easily. Love like this doesn't come along very often."

He kisses my forehead, and then he and Andy are gone, headed back to the house that chills me to the bone.

"Come on, child," Sophia says from behind me. She doesn't startle me; I felt her approach. "Let's get to work."

"He didn't exactly say it back to me," I remark as we climb the stairs.

"If you can't see the love in his eyes when he looks at you, you're as blind as Stevie Wonder, my sweet girl."

"It's time."

I turn to see my sisters waiting for me on the threshold of the guest room at Miss Sophia's house. We all worked well into the night. All of the others went home to rest, leaving just the three of us with Miss Sophia.

She wanted to keep us here last night, to protect and watch over us.

I nod and swallow hard. I'm not nearly as nervous as

I was last night. Somewhere around three in the morning, a calm washed over me, leaving me feeling confident and secure in the knowledge that although tonight will be a fight, we will win.

Everything *will* be okay.

I have to believe that.

"Have you heard from Cash?" Daphne asks as we walk into the kitchen and drink the potions Miss Sophia set out for us.

"Yes, he's meeting us over there. They got that basement room cleared out early this morning, and we've been given full ownership as of about an hour ago."

"And the body?"

"It'll be there," I confirm.

Miss Sophia left before us, so the three of us drive to Horace's house together. I don't even glance down the road to Mama's. I've barely spared her a thought since all of this began.

We pull in behind another car and get out. The building is already surrounded by all of the witches that were at Miss Sophia's house throughout the night, along with others I don't know.

"She called in reinforcements," I mutter.

"There can be no mistakes on this one," Miss Sophia says as she joins us. "I need a word with just the three of you before we begin."

"What's wrong?"

She looks worried. "I shouldn't tell you this. Giving you information about what's to come isn't safe and isn't what I normally do. But I also don't want to give you false hope. What we do here today is important and will extinguish this evil one's light for a while."

We glance at each other.

"For *a while*?" I ask.

"Yes. His spirit is stronger than any other I've seen. His will is unmatched. So, yes, we will break him here today, but in order for it to be permanent, there will be steps that can't be taken at this time. That's all I can tell you."

"The six," I murmur. "Are not ready."

Her eyes hold mine. "That's right."

A truck pulls in right behind us, interrupting us, and Cash hops out of the passenger seat. He rushes to me and holds me close, and I immediately feel more at ease.

"How are you, babe?"

I smile against his chest. "I'm much better now. Did you get any rest?"

"I'll rest tomorrow." He kisses my cheek, then motions to Andy. "The boys are going to set the body in the house. Is there anywhere specific you want him?"

"I'm in charge of that," Daphne says. "The answer is *yes*, and I will be able to feel where is best."

Daphne joins Andy and the others, and just as I turn to the house, the front door opens, and we all pause.

"Git outta here!"

"Mama?" I frown, not believing my eyes. "Mama, what are you doing here?"

"Y'all needta git!" She hoists a broom with one hand, and in the other, she holds...a hand.

A shadow's hand.

"Everyone stop," I order, raising my arm. Miss Sophia joins me.

"He has her, child," she says softly.

"I see him." Before my eyes, he changes from a shadow to an apparition. He holds Mama's hand and smiles in that evil, sick way of his. "Does he think he can hold her hostage?"

"Ask him," Millie suggests.

"Horace, I don't know what you're doing with my mother, but it won't work."

He doesn't reply. He simply moves behind her and wraps his arms around her chest. Suddenly, hundreds of shadows pour out of the house, flanking him, joining him as they wrap my mother in evil. She cries out as if she's in pain.

"That's enough," I yell. "You're acting like a child who didn't get his way!"

"Circle the house," Miss Sophia instructs everyone. "Get in your places! The moon is rising. It's time."

I turn to Andy. "Put him on the porch. Uncover him."

Andy nods. He can't see Horace and the shadows, he can only see Mama, shrieking in pain. Andy sets Horace's body on the porch, uncovers it, and hurries back down the steps.

Shadows try to follow him, but Sophia circled the

house with salt before we arrived, and it serves as a barrier, holding the evil inside.

The chanting begins from the side of the house and then spreads around the structure counterclockwise. The witches behind the house sit and stand in boats, linking themselves together by holding hands.

The shadows cover the house now, a spectral pile of death.

The chanting grows louder.

The wind picks up, swirling through our hair, tugging at our clothes. The chanting is loud so it can be heard over the wind, fueled by magic and might.

Lightning strikes the house, setting it ablaze. I watch as Horace's face distorts into rage and fear, and my eyes hold his.

"You're going to hell, you son of a bitch."

The fire engulfs the house, and the shadows shriek, retreating as quickly as they appeared.

"Don't break the circle!" Sophia yells to me, but I shake my head.

"I can't let her burn to death!"

I run over the salt, and immediately feel the heat of the fire. The shrieking gets louder.

Suddenly, I'm pulled inside, held by meaty arms with the face of the devil snarling at me.

"I've got you, you little bitch. I may not get your sisters, but you're mine. You think you can hurt me?"

He slaps me, sending me to the floor.

It's so hot.

I'm going to burn in here.

"I can't believe you're such an ungrateful little bitch." He kicks me, making me cough in pain. "I'm going to kill you. I'm not going to make it beautiful like I planned before."

He fists my hair and lifts me high off the floor. It feels like my skin is melting off my body, the air is so hot.

"Brielle!"

Cash!

"You ruined everything," Horace says and slams me to the floor again. It's hard to breathe. I can't see. But I can hear Cash calling my name.

"You're not going to kill me." My voice is a croak. Suddenly, Cash is standing next to me, his hand around mine. "We're going to destroy you!"

I begin my own chant. I can hear the others, their voices rising up around us, and as the words leave my mouth, Cash carries me out of the house. He grabs Mama's hand as we pass her and drags her with us.

Once we're on the other side of the salt barrier, the flames turn red, then blue, and rise up to the night sky, almost blinding us with their light. The explosion is fierce and bright, and then, as quickly as it started, the wind is gone, and the shadows shriek one last time before evaporating into the air. The black particles float up into the sky and disappear.

"She's burned," someone says, and I glance around, wondering who they're talking about.

"Brielle." I turn to look at Cash. "Honey, you're burned. We need to get you to the hospital."

"What about you?"

He shakes his head. "I ran in and out."

"It felt like you were in there forever." I swallow and turn to find my mother sitting not far away, looking around as if she's just woken from a dream.

"Brielle?" she asks. "Where are we?"

I look at Cash and frown.

"We're at Horace's house. Or what's left of it."

"Horace?" She frowns, and then her eyes fill with fear. "He's a bad man. A bad, bad man."

"He's not here."

Millie and Daphne join us. Miss Sophia, Lena, and Mal are close by. The others are still chanting, casting spells and cleaning up.

"Don't know how I got here," Mama says. "The voices stopped talking."

"The voices?" Daphne asks.

Mama nods, and then her eyes fill with tears. "You're all grown up. When did you grow up?"

"We grew up a long time ago," Millie reminds her.

"She's confused," I say as Miss Sophia joins us, but she shakes her head.

"I don't think so. Not in the way you mean. Ruth, what's the last thing you remember?"

"Well, I don't know. I remember their daddy hitting me. Harder than the times before."

I feel my eyes go wide.

"And then he was gone. Everyone was gone. And I was left in the house. Every time I tried to leave, I went away again."

"Oh my gods." I stand and reach for her. "They kept you there."

"Who?" she asks, then frames my face with her frail hands. "Oh, you are a beauty, aren't you?"

"I wish I'd known," Miss Sophia says. "Ruth, I'm so very sorry. I had no idea that you were a prisoner in your own house."

"There was a woman, in the rocking chair." Mama's eyes are blue and clear as day as she smiles. "She kept me company."

The rocking chair.

Could it be that the one spirit that wasn't evil was the one in that chair?

Was she protecting her?

"Let's go, ladies," Cash says, wrapping his arm around my shoulders. "We need to get these burns checked out."

I nod but keep my mother in sight all the way to the hospital.

"So, LET ME GET THIS STRAIGHT," Millie says in the morning, sitting next to my bed at the hospital. "Our mother *isn't* an evil human being, but it was the evil spirits in the house that made her that way? And kept her there? And, Horace, along with his terrible mother, were behind it all?"

"Well, we can't prove that they were behind it," Millie says. "But I know because I dropped my shields long enough to look. Horace helped. He kept the bad spirits there, to keep an eye on us. He had a thing for Mama, and she *did* play with him a lot, so she's not completely innocent."

"Well that's...disturbing," I whisper. My throat hurts from the heat and smoke I inhaled in the house. "What happens to her now?"

"She'll be in the mental hospital for quite some time," Cash says as he walks into the room. "I just spoke with her doctor. He'll be in soon to talk to all of you."

"You know, I've said it before, and I'll say it again," Millie says. "She may not be the salt of the earth kind of mother, but no one deserves that kind of torment."

"I wonder if she was possessed when she killed our father," I say, frowning. "I mean, she doesn't even *sound* the same, right? Her accent, the way she phrases things, it's so different from how she sounded when we saw her just a couple of weeks ago."

"It honestly could be," Daphne says. "I'm sure we can ask Miss Sophia more questions later. She went home to rest."

"Everyone sure supported us," I say. "The whole thing was just amazing."

"Witches aren't always scary," Millie says with a wink. "And they look after their own."

CHAPTER TWENTY-SEVEN
Brielle

"It's about time we took this day," Cash says as he passes me a bowl of freshly popped corn and cozies up with me on the couch. "I mean, you're not naked, but it's close."

"I can't be naked all the livelong day," I remind him and push a handful of popcorn into my mouth.

"You're such a lady, darlin'," he says on a laugh, so I toss a kernel his way, which he eats.

"You can get me naked later." I haven't said anything to him yet, but there's a new shadow in my apartment today. It's not malicious. On the contrary, actually.

But it's not my place to say anything.

So, I've steered him away from sex and instead suggested that we curl up on the couch with a Marvel movie, while we wait for the call that's about to come.

We don't wait long.

"Hello?" he says into the phone. "Hey, Felicia. How are things?"

He sits up and sets the bowl aside before pushing his hand through his hair. I rub his back in big, soothing circles.

"I see. No, I know there's nothing you could have done, sweetheart. I'm so grateful that you were there, and I know Andy is, too. He'll be happy to have you home soon, but I'll talk to him today, and he and I will come to you tonight or tomorrow. No, you don't have to do all of that by yourself, we'll be there. Thank you, Felicia. We owe you big time. Love you, too. Okay, bye."

He hangs up and sighs deeply. "My mom passed away today."

"Yeah." I lean in to kiss his shoulder. "I know."

He frowns down at me. "How do you know?"

"I, uh—"

"Right." He nods once and scratches the back of his neck. "Is she here now?"

"She is. I can't see her face, she's just a shadow. But I can tell it's her."

He bites his lip and then stands to pace the living room.

"Mom, I have some things to tell you. First of all, I'm sorry that I wasn't there these past few weeks. I know you enjoyed having Felicia with you, and she loves you a lot, but it should have been me, and I apologize for that."

"She's shaking her head at you."

Cash laughs. "Yeah, she would." He turns to me, his green eyes suddenly alight with humor. "Mom, I have to tell you about something else. I met this girl, and you'd like her a lot. She's funny. She's close to her family, so that's nice, and she has some quirks, but hell, who doesn't, right?

"She has blue eyes that just reach in and grab hold of your heart. I was hoping to introduce you to her in Savannah, but this'll do, I guess. Because you see, Mom, I love Brielle, and I'm going to ask her to marry me."

My heart stills in my chest, but I don't say anything. I just watch him as he tells his mom all about me.

"She doesn't know yet, of course. I know it means that some things will have to change with my job, and where my home base is, but I like it in New Orleans, and it'll be nice to be close to Andy most of the time. I think you'd approve of that."

I clear my throat. "She nodded."

"I just don't think I can go through life without her, Mom. She's incredible. So, I'm going to stay here, marry her, and have some babies. Who would have thought? I certainly didn't."

"She just raised her hand." I can't help but laugh.

"Of course, you knew." His eyes fill with sorrow now. "Man, I'm going to miss you, Mom. I wish I'd said these things when you were still here, but I guess this'll have to do. I'll take care of Andy and Felicia. And Brielle, too. You don't have to worry about anything. I love you, Mom."

I brush at a tear on my cheek. "She blew you a kiss, and she's gone."

He nods. "Wow, this is weird. But good. Thank you for that."

"You're welcome."

"I meant it. Every word of it."

He scoops me into his lap and buries his face in my neck. "You're my home, Brielle. You have been since the first moment I laid eyes on you. Marry me. Have a family with me."

"Yeah." I kiss his cheek. "I think that's a good idea."

He grins.

"It's a damn good idea."

"I can't wait to tell my sisters. We get to plan a wedding!"

"Let's keep it just between us for a little while."

"For how long?"

"Just an hour." He grins and lifts me, headed for the bedroom. "Maybe two."

EPILOGUE

Millie

"A spring wedding." I take a deep breath and let it out slowly, grinning like a loon. "Oh, that sounds so lovely."

"Especially in New Orleans," Daphne agrees. "Do you have a venue yet?"

"I haven't even started thinking about it," Brielle replies. "I mean, he just asked me yesterday."

"I'm sure sorry about his mama," I say. "That's so sad. But you gave him an awesome gift of getting to talk to her before she moved on."

"He seems pretty at peace with it all," Brielle says. "Sure, he's sad, but that's to be expected. I think she was sick for quite a while. That's why his sister-in-law was out to check on her."

"That makes sense," I say. "Still sad, though. I'll whip them up a soothing potion to help them feel better."

"You're sweet," Brielle says. "Thank you."

"Well, they're family now," I remind her. "What kind of flowers are you going to have? I think you should have some wisteria. And lilacs. Camelia is a must."

"No roses," Daphne says, shaking her head. "If I never see a rose again, it'll be too soon."

"I always meant to ask and kept forgetting," Brielle says to our sister. "What did you see when you touched the rose at Mama's house that day."

Daphne frowns and swallows hard. "Nothing."

"Lies," Brielle and I say in unison.

"We're talking about your *wedding*," Daphne says. "I don't want to talk about creepy, horrible things. I'll just confirm that the man who fathered us is buried in that spot. And it was his spirit that haunted the hell out of us for years."

"Well, we knew that." I bite my thumbnail the way I always do when I'm deep in thought. "Do you think the evil spirits in that house made him mean? Or do you think he started out that way, and the spirits fed on his cruelty?"

"Maybe both," Brielle says with a shrug. "I don't think Mama started out mean, but she was a victim of the evil in the house. As for him? Who knows? It could have been a combination of the two."

"Have either of you been to see her?" Daphne asks.

"I went," I say, surprising them both. "She recognized me, and she seems to be doing better. But she has a long road ahead."

"Okay, enough about that," Daphne says. "Who's going to be your maid of honor?"

"What do you mean?" Brielle frowns. "I have two. Both of you will do it. I could never choose between you."

"That's sweet."

"And we accept," Daphne adds, laughing. "Millie, we should toast with some champagne."

"I have the perfect bottle," I say as I stand and head for the kitchen. "I got it a couple of months ago. And, no, I haven't put any potions inside it. Yet."

"Shocker," Brielle says with a laugh. "I think we can be without a potion just this once. Hey, speaking of, you didn't give a love potion to Cash, did you?"

"Nope, he loves you all on his own. He didn't need me for that."

I open the fridge and reach for the bubbly, then stop cold.

There's a small cup of blood sitting right in the middle of the center shelf.

"Hey, guys?"

"Yeah?" they say in unison.

"Where did this come from?"

ABOUT SPELLS

From New York Times Bestselling Author, Kristen Proby, comes Spells, the next installment in her gripping Bayou Magic series...

As a powerful hedgewitch and psychic, there isn't much I can't work to my advantage and finesse with a spell. Love, fortune, and even the perfect cup of coffee are all possible with the snap of my fingers.

But some things are utterly beyond my control.

Like the powerful and broody warlock who's been a part of my life for as long as I can remember—and even the lifetimes I often can't. Things almost as dangerous as Lucien Bergeron's hold on me and the breathtaking smiles only I get to see.

Or the evil still stalking the streets of New Orleans that beckons to me to see. To feel. To die.

With everything riding on a razors-edge, and things that have been portended coming to fruition, threatening both me and those I love, I'm not sure if I'm strong enough to resist my fate. Or his charm.

If I work with Lucien, it could mean the end for both of us.

If I don't, those I love most will pay.

SPELLS RELEASES ON OCTOBER 29, 2020. You can preorder on all retailers here:

www.kristenprobyauthor.com/spells

ABOUT THE AUTHOR

Kristen Proby has published close to fifty titles, many of which have hit the USA Today, New York Times and Wall Street Journal Bestsellers lists. She continues to self publish, best known for her With Me In Seattle and Boudreaux series, and is also proud to work with William Morrow, a division of HarperCollins, with the Fusion and Romancing Manhattan Series.

Kristen and her husband, John, make their home in her hometown of Whitefish, Montana with their two cats and dog.

facebook.com/booksbykristenproby
instagram.com/kristenproby
bookbub.com/profile/kristen-proby
goodreads.com/kristenproby

NEWSLETTER SIGN UP

I hope you enjoyed reading this story as much as I enjoyed writing it! For upcoming book news, be sure to join my newsletter! I promise I will only send you news-filled mail, and none of the spam. You can sign up here:

https://mailchi.mp/kristenproby.com/
newsletter-sign-up

ALSO BY KRISTEN PROBY:

Other Books by Kristen Proby

The With Me In Seattle Series

Come Away With Me
Under The Mistletoe With Me
Fight With Me
Play With Me
Rock With Me
Safe With Me
Tied With Me
Breathe With Me
Forever With Me
Stay With Me
Indulge With Me
Love With Me
Dance With Me

Dream With Me

Coming in 2020:
You Belong With Me
Imagine With Me
Shine With Me

Check out the full series here: https://www.
kristenprobyauthor.com/with-me-in-seattle

The Big Sky Universe

Love Under the Big Sky

Loving Cara
Seducing Lauren
Falling for Jillian
Saving Grace

The Big Sky

Charming Hannah
Kissing Jenna
Waiting for Willa
Soaring With Fallon

Big Sky Royal

Enchanting Sebastian
Enticing Liam

Coming in 2020:

Taunting Callum

Check out the full Big Sky universe here: https://
www.kristenprobyauthor.com/under-the-big-sky

Bayou Magic

Shadows

Coming in 2020:
Spells

Check out the full series here: https://www.
kristenprobyauthor.com/bayou-magic

The Romancing Manhattan Series

All the Way
All it Takes

Coming in 2020
After All

Check out the full series here: https://www.
kristenprobyauthor.com/romancing-manhattan

The Boudreaux Series

Easy Love

ALSO BY KRISTEN PROBY:

Easy Charm

Easy Melody

Easy Kisses

Easy Magic

Easy Fortune

Easy Nights

Check out the full series here: https://www.
kristenprobyauthor.com/boudreaux

The Fusion Series

Listen to Me

Close to You

Blush for Me

The Beauty of Us

Savor You

Check out the full series here: https://www.
kristenprobyauthor.com/fusion

From 1001 Dark Nights

Easy With You

Easy For Keeps

No Reservations

Tempting Brooke

Wonder With Me

Coming in 2020:
Shine With Me

Kristen Proby's Crossover Collection

Soaring with Fallon, A Big Sky Novel

Wicked Force: A Wicked Horse Vegas/Big Sky Novella
By Sawyer Bennett

All Stars Fall: A Seaside Pictures/Big Sky Novella
By Rachel Van Dyken

Hold On: A Play On/Big Sky Novella
By Samantha Young

Worth Fighting For: A Warrior Fight Club/Big Sky
Novella
By Laura Kaye

Crazy Imperfect Love: A Dirty Dicks/Big Sky Novella
By K.L. Grayson

Nothing Without You: A Forever Yours/Big Sky Novella
By Monica Murphy

Check out the entire Crossover Collection here:
https://www.kristenprobyauthor.com/kristen-proby-
crossover-collection

Made in the USA
Columbia, SC
21 October 2020